Also by Sophie Mouette

Novels

Cat Scratch Fever
Out of the Frying Pan
Possessed, Undressed, and in a Mess

Short Stories

Catalyst
Don't Move
Dyeing for Her
Hidden Treasure
Sacred Places
Under a Double Rainbow

Praise for Andrea Dale

"Legendary erotica heavy-hitter."

—über-legendary Violet Blue

"Incredibly erotic."

—Erotica-Readers.com

["The Queen of Christmas" is] "as perfect a blend of sex and humor as rum-spiked eggnog."

—Donna George Storey,
author of *Amorous Woman*

Praise for Teresa Noelle Roberts

"['Waiting for Ilya'] was a tender and heartwarming story … [that] shows what can be done in a good romance for a married couple."

—The Itinerant Librarian

"The kink and sex between Selene and Nick was scrumptious and had me turning virtual page after page [of *Knowing the Ropes*]."

—Fallen Angel Reviews

"Teresa has a wonderful sense of humor and isn't afraid to use it to get her character's points across."

—Beth Wylde
author of *Women Gone Wylde*

Sexy
in Your
Stocking
❦

Twelve Erotic Tales for the Holidays

LKP
LITTLE KISSES
PRESS

Sexy in Your Stocking:
Twelve Erotic Tales for the Holidays
Andrea Dale, Teresa Noelle Roberts, Sophie Mouette

Print edition published 2013 by Little Kisses Press

First Edition
ISBN-13: 978-0615921914
ISBN-10: 0615921914

Inquiries should be addressed to
Little Kisses Press
littlekissespress@gmail.com
http://www.littlekissespress.com

Cover image from TheresaTibbetts / iStockphoto
Cover and logo designed by Dayle Dermatis

Table of Contents

Introduction 1

Andrea Dale

The Queen of Christmas 3
Frozen 13
On the Twelfth Day 21
Let It Snow 29
Santa Claus is Comin' 39
Mrs. Claus and the Naughty Elf 49

Teresa Noelle Roberts

Christmas Blizzard 55
Happy Krampusnacht 81
Running Away From Christmas 89

Sophie Mouette

A Bird in the Hand 99
Bringing Back the Light… 105
Hidden Treasure 11

Sexy
in Your
Stocking

☙

Twelve Erotic Tales for the Holidays

Introduction

About ten years ago (egads!) Andrea and Teresa decided to write a story together for an anthology of lesbian holiday erotica. Andrea proposed an idea, but Teresa didn't believe that snow could be sexy, so Andrea dove in to prove her wrong. Halfway through the story, however, the entire thing unfolded in front of Andrea's eyes, so she called Teresa and asked if she could take it as a solo story. Teresa, always gracious, agreed.

Andrea was nonetheless sad that they weren't writing the story together, but happily, they went on to write many more stories together as Sophie Mouette (as well as separately), and thus this collection of erotic holiday stories came together.

But really, why do we write so many holiday stories?

The holidays make great story fodder because they're so emotionally charged. The winter holidays are a season of festivity, colored lights, beloved music, great food, family rituals, and resonant tales, both religious stories and secular ones about Santa and the Grinch. They're also highly stressful, crazy busy, and often fraught with unrealistic expectations and family drama. Lost loves and absent friends and family cast long shadows. And of course the holidays fall at what's literally the darkest time of year if you live north of the Equator—probably the reason so many of these midwinter holidays are festivals of light. With all those emotions at play, it's easy to create dramatic situations that lead, first to conflict, then to expressions of love and lust.

But by the same token, holiday stories can be fun! When else can you write about sexy Santa Clauses or naughty games with icicles, or get unabashedly sentimental as well as sexy? And there are all those long, dark nights to heat up....

Whether you celebrate Christmas or Hanukah or the Solstice or Kwanzaa or everything or nothing at all, we hope the joy and magic of the season finds you naked under mistletoe or snuggly blankets (or on a sunny Caribbean beach!) with someone who drives you crazy with lust.

—Andrea Dale,
Teresa Noelle Roberts,
& Sophie Mouette

Andrea Dale

�

The Queen of Christmas

They called me the Queen of Christmas. I *am* the Queen of Christmas.

I was the one who organized the carolers in full, proper Victorian clothing. I was the one who welcomed other caroling groups with wassail, candy canes, and stockings (lovingly hand-embroidered) stuffed with goodies. I was the one who liberated the Nativity scene that the city was retiring, so I was the one with life-sized camels in my front yard. I was the one with the lighted, moving reindeer on the roof and the Santa who moved up and down the chimney.

People came from miles around to see what the Queen of Christmas had in store this year.

That is, until *he* moved across the street.

He went pretty elaborate for Halloween, and I thought, fine, that's your holiday. But then Christmas rolled around.

At first, his display seemed innocuous. Mostly lights—lots of them, but all white. He might illuminate the neighborhood like it was midday, but all the better to see my yard, you know?

Then one night I heard the music. He'd cleverly hidden some impressive speakers in the bushes, because I could hear it with the window closed and the carols on my own stereo. So help me, my china rattled.

We've all seen the Tran-Siberian Orchestra house, right? He'd recreated the damn thing. Yeah, it was impressive. But it was seriously detracting from my own decorations.

So I went over there and hammered on his front door, making his cranberry-and-ivy wreath bounce against the wood.

"Oh, hey, Shelly," he said.

Of course he knew who I was. On December first, I deliver plates of hand-decorated sugar cookies to everyone in the neighborhood, and then, on the fifth, a schedule of all of the local schools' pageants and concerts, printed on fir-scented paper. On the fifteenth, gingerbread men and eggnog. On the twenty-first, Solstice candles, and at the appropriate time, oil for Chanukah. (Never let it be said I don't respect all of the winter holidays.)

See, now here's the other problem. I've had my eye on Bradley St. Clair since the moment he moved into the neighborhood. He's one yummy-looking man, and he had my panties damp from the start. I'd done some flirting, but I was waiting to make my move until after Twelfth Night, when things calmed down again. That didn't mean I hadn't masturbated more than once thinking about him, and I'd even dusted off a pair of binoculars to find how much I could see across the street.

Sadly, his bedroom was at the back of the house, and I was *not* enough of a peeping Tom to hide in his backyard bushes.

Right now, he had on a long underwear top with a convenient tear highlighting his chest, and faded jeans that molded to his muscular thighs. Casual, but oh-so-sexy. He had a snifter of brandy in one hand, and his dark hair was rumpled.

For a long moment, I forgot why I'd stormed over here. I forgot that I'd stormed, even. I was too busy staring at him, my nipples at greater attention than the tin soldiers in "The Nutcracker." Salute me, baby.

Then I realized he was talking, and I couldn't hear him over that damnable music.

"Turn it down," I shouted.

"What? Oh, right." He turned a knob just inside the front door, and the orchestra from hell went down a few thousand decibels.

"C'mon in," he said. "Want some brandy?"

Well, damn, I wasn't about to turn that down.

"That's some display," I said as he poured my drink. I meant the lights and music, but the sight of his fine ass as he bent over to pick up the cap he'd dropped was something to behold.

"Thanks," he said. He handed me the drink and sat down next to me. He smelled kind of pine-y, kind of cinnamon-y. Like Christmas. I squirmed in my seat. It was hot in here, and not just from the fire crackling in the fireplace.

"I've been working on the specs for a couple of years," he said. "The electrical engineering degree finally came in handy for something interesting."

"It's really loud," I said, cursing myself for sounding like someone's mother at a rock concert.

"Yeah, sorry about that. I'm still working out the details. I didn't realize how far it was carrying." He didn't look abashed or repentant, although I didn't doubt the sincerity of his apology. He was simply acknowledging his mistake, confident that he could fix it.

Maybe it was the brandy, or the heat off his tight bod, or the glint of a tiny gold hoop in his right ear. Whatever. I accepted his apology, and I don't remember much of the conversation after that. Something about our mutual love of the season. He liked my chimney-climbing Santa, was impressed by my mechanical ability. Cool. Go me. Do you mind if I lean in and just inhale you?

I caught myself before I did anything stupid. I had the holidays to get through before I could allow myself to go into full-on seduction mode. And besides, he was still pissing me off a little.

Best intentions and all that. I was standing in his foyer, pulling on my faux-fur-cuffed leather gloves for the chilly tromp across the street, when I clued in to his wolfish grin.

"What?"

He tilted his head up.

I followed his gaze, and saw the mistletoe dangling from the amber Arts-and-Crafts light fixture. Aw, hell.

He kissed with the same confidence he'd had when talking about his engineering expertise. One hand loosely threaded through my hair, keeping me against him. His lips moved against mine, his teeth nipping my lower lip and then his tongue darting out to soothe.

I felt that kiss all the way down to my clit, and then some.

I was pretty much ready to hop up and wrap my legs around his waist in preparation for him carrying me off to some soft surface where he could ring my jingle bells, when he eased away.

"Happy holidays, Shelly," he said.

Oh yeah, they were happy, all right. And once they were over…

*

Once they were over, I was simply going to have to kill him. Call it the candy cane defense.

True to his word, Brad kept the music to a reasonable level. His impressive decorations had something to do with the increase in the number of people visiting our street, and it irked the hell out of me to stand on my front porch in a holly-patterned apron with a tray of green-and-red sparkled cupcakes and face everyone's *backs*.

And then there was the line to get into his backyard. What in Jesus' birthday was *that* all about?

I'll tell you. I went over and found out he'd set up a whole Santa's Grotto, and dressed himself as Santa. He had a huge bag of gifts, and he didn't discriminate about who got them.

That wasn't all. He had a slide—a *slide*—for kids to skim down to land right next to ol' Santa.

He had completely, utterly, totally gazumped everything I'd ever done.

And he was going to pay.

*

In my defense, he started it. It was his mistletoe, and *he* kissed *me*.

That's what gave me the idea. I had to find a way through his defenses; I had to hit him where it hurt. Which was, I realized, was below the belt.

Santa could not work effectively with a boner, is what I'm saying.

I went for less of a Mrs. Claus look and more of a Santa's helper theme. Skimpy white-fur-trimmed, red stretch velvet top and flippy short velvet skirt. Wide black belt cinching my waist in an attractive fashion. Black fencenet thigh-highs and short black boots with a sassy heel.

To top it all off, a perky Santa hat with a pin that said "Mistletoe: Kiss Below."

The plan was simple: Distract him, and them offer him the goods only if he backed down from the contest. Hopefully it wouldn't take too long, because in this outfit, I was going to freeze my cute buns off very quickly.

I loaded up a basket of cookies and made my way across the street, my boots crunching in the snow at the curb. There was a line of people all down the sidewalk, waiting to get back there. I smiled at them and they parted to let me through, probably assuming I was part of the show.

I waited until a kid came out of the grotto, and popped inside before Brad could call for the next one to come down the slide.

"Shelly!" He stood when he saw me. "I'd say 'ho ho ho,' but I wouldn't want you to take it the wrong way."

"You like it?" I asked, pirouetting to give him a full view.

"I do indeed," he said. "I just don't get it. Why are you here? It's been obvious that you view me as the competition, that you can't stand anyone having what might be construed as a bigger or better holiday display."

I'd always thought jaw-dropping was a cliché, but mine did. I'd had no freaking clue he knew how I felt.

"I've always had the house everyone talks about," I said. "It's my *thing*. I'm sick of you taking away from that."

He shook his head. Even with the padded suit and the wig and the poufy white eyebrows, he was still majorly hot, and that tingle I was feeling wasn't from the cold. "Shelly, Christmas is about sharing, about giving. Not about competition."

"So back off."

"Can't we both have great displays?"

Dammit, I didn't want him to be reasonable. It made me feel unreasonable. And unseasonable. "No," I said stubbornly.

I knew I was being pouty. I knew I deserved coal in my stocking. But I was still surprised when Brad snatched me up and sat down on his throne with me head-down and ass-up.

I started to say something about this not being the appropriate way to sit on Santa's lap when his hand connected with my now-very-vulnerable ass.

I squealed as the pain and heat seared through me, knowing it was worse because my flesh was cold.

"Careful," Brad said, his voice low and dark and dangerous. "You don't want the kiddies outside to hear."

Crap. As stubborn as I am, it's still about Christmas, and there was no way I'd risk spoiling Christmas for children.

I squirmed, but I couldn't get any purchase, and Brad's other hand was firmly in the small of my back.

Another sharp smack, and I wondered whether that was audible over the cheerful holiday music. I assumed not, or he would've stopped. Somehow, I trusted that.

His hand came down on my ass again. I'd received play-spankings from partners in the past, but they'd never been my be-all, end-all.

This was entirely different.

Maybe it was the music, or the smell of spiced eggnog, or the crisp winter air. It was probably all of those things. It was definitely the fact that it was Santa's lap on which I was being thoroughly put in my place.

Three spanks in, and I was completely, irretrievably aroused. Nipples hard like last year's fruitcake, my red stretch-lace panties drenched and my clit buzzing.

"Twelve," I dimly heard Brad say. "One for each day of Christmas."

Slap, slap, slap, and I was sure my ass was as red as the panties that covered it. I wanted him to pull them down; I wanted him to smell my arousal. I wanted him to search out my clit with his fingers and bring me over the edge, which I was sure would take only a stroke or two.

In the final flurry of smacks, I thought I might even come without the benefit of that. So close…

He stopped. Dammit. I could feel his erection pressing against my belly.

"Brad…"

"The kids are waiting, Shelly." He helped me to my feet, even though the last thing I wanted to do was stand up, and pointed to the basket of cookies I'd brought. "You can hand those out once they tell me what they want."

My cheeks flamed as red as my ass. He expected me to stand here, desperate for release, and make nice to the children as if nothing was going on?

Apparently so. Because he grinned that wolfish grin and added, "Then I'll give you what you really want."

He grabbed the pillow he'd used to cushion the wooden throne's seat and plopped it on his lap. Smart guy. Resourceful. Damn him.

No matter how much I resented him right now, I wanted my gift from Santa in the worst way. So I smiled and handed out cookies, constantly, achingly aware of the slickness between my thighs with every movement I made.

The kids were thrilled. Cranky as I was, I could see that. And a kid thrilled from meeting Santa went a long way to warm the cockles of the Queen of Christmas's heart. What could I do but succumb, even if I had to clutch the basket against my chest so they couldn't see my protruding nubs, even as I prayed the scent of gingerbread masked the scent of my own arousal.

By the time the last child toddled out of the grotto, I was light-headed from Christmas joy and joyous, desperate arousal.

"Wait here," Brad said. "I'll be right back."

Wait, longer? I almost fainted from the thought. But I realized he was turning off the lights, making it clear that Santa's Grotto wasn't taking any new requests.

He reached for me, but I had other plans. Even as he kissed me hard enough to make my head spin like a dreidel, I nudged him backwards until he was sitting on the throne again.

"You said Christmas was about giving, right?" I said, burrowing through the layers of padding and finally, blissfully, drawing out his cock. I sucked it like it was a candy cane and I was the starving Little Match Girl. I could've sworn he tasted like peppermint. I know he felt really good in my mouth, hard and sweet, and that his moans wove through and counterpointed the carols over the sound system like the tenor solo at church.

How could I never have come up with this kink before? Blowing Santa was bringing me closer to climax than being spanked by him.

We were both on the verge when, somehow, he found the strength to ease me off his cock. I whimpered with displeasure, but when he arranged me on my knees on the throne, my hands gripping the arm rests, I stopped complaining. I wiggled my ass invitingly, gazing over my shoulder at him.

He didn't need further invitation.

He sank into me, and when the crisp rough curls of his hair scraped against my sore spanked ass, a shudder convulsed me. Not quite an orgasm, but something just as powerful.

Call it the Spirit of Christmas. All I knew is that when Brad started thrusting, I knew the Queen of Christmas had met her match.

Frozen

Becca wanted to get a tree on December first.

I tried to talk her out of it, but she was having none of that. Her father had a tree farm in the mountains, she said, and when she was a kid she'd always been the one to pick out their family tree. Now, he continued to give her one for free—and she wanted to beat the rush and get the absolute best one possible.

I, on the other hand, wasn't even sure if I'd still be around on the twenty-fifth. I went with her, because I couldn't resist that adorable uptilted nose and the dimple on her left cheek, but I made no promises otherwise.

It had snowed on and off since early November, and the world was white and eerily silent except for the sound of our boots crunching through the frozen cover. Beneath the tall pines, all lined up stately and proud, the snow cover was thinner, and occasionally I scuffed up enough to see the brown needles and dirt beneath.

"It's not normal," I said for what seemed like the hundredth time. "This white stuff falling from the sky at regular intervals. You should be able to visit winter, and then go home."

Becca laughed and kissed my cheek, her lips warm against the flesh that was reddened by the cold. "Oh, you California girl, you," she said. "How can it be the holidays without snow?"

It was a familiar argument, with no underlying malice or anger. We were just from very different places, and teased it other about it.

A few moments later I realized we'd left the carefully planted rows of trees and had headed on a slight incline, through birches and firs and other trees I couldn't quite identify, all more jumbled together. I pointed out our misdirection.

"Oh, I know," she said. "We never get our own tree from the farm proper. My dad owns acres and acres here, and it's our tradition that we get our tree from farther back."

I bit back a sigh, wistfully imagining a steaming cup of hot chocolate laced with crème de menthe. Shoving my hands in my pockets, I followed Becca deeper into the wintry woods.

It wasn't much of a problem following her, actually, because I could focus on her sweet ass, contained in a pair of tight jeans (with silk long underwear beneath, I happened to know, having been involved in making it difficult for her to keep them on earlier today). Right now, there wasn't anything I wanted more to be in a nice warm bed with her, my hands cupping that tight bottom as I buried my head between her thighs and made her wail as she came.

I loved the sweet taste of her slippery folds, like cinnamon, and how they turned so dark when she was aroused, fiery red like the rest of her. Afterwards I'd kiss away the orgasmic flush from her delicate breasts, only to be unable to resist taking one of her pert nipples in my mouth, and then we'd be starting all over again…

The trees thinned as we walked, and Becca paused to let me catch up, slipping her hand into mine. The intimacy of the action, despite the layers of knitted wool between our fingers, touched me. We'd been dating for seven months now, living together for two-and-a-half, and yet I was still surprised by the tenderness. I felt guilty, too—after Lindy's death, I didn't think I'd ever open up to anyone like that again.

I hadn't intended to move in with Becca, exactly, but the lease ran out on the apartment I was subletting and Becca had a spare room. Not that I ever slept in it, mind you—we set up the other room as a studio for me and an office for her.

I'd fled California when Lindy died after four years of living and loving together. I immersed myself in grad school in Minneapolis, as different a place as I could find, and that's where I'd met Becca.

We'd started out talking about architecture, and tumbled into bed not long after that. When she was through stunning me with her energy and inventiveness and I'd caught my breath, we went right back to talking…and then right back into screwing again.

I never stopped missing Lindy, but when I was tangled and sweaty with Becca, the pain lessened. She had that effect on me—perhaps because she was so unreserved, so delightfully free.

I made Becca no promises, knowing she deserved more than I could give her. But when I tried to tell her that, Becca would shake her head, brushing her silken red hair across my face, and tell me that our time together was all that mattered.

"We're only given a certain amount of time on this earth," she'd say. "Use every moment wisely, to the greatest extent that you can."

I was afraid Becca would fall in love with me, and I'd have to leave. But right now, I was trying to live in the moment. Even if it was a very chilly one.

We came to a clearing, a circle of trees with the snow untouched in the center.

"So beautiful," Becca breathed. "So pure."

"It *is* pretty," I agreed reluctantly. "Pristine. Like we're the first people to come here."

She kissed me again, this time on the lips, her tongue caressing. Then she pulled back, and I saw a mischievous glint in her eyes.

"Snow angels!" she shouted, her voice startling a cardinal into a flutter of crimson. She grabbed my hand again and dragged me into the center of the clearing. Flinging herself down on her back, she waved her arms and legs frantically.

"Are you having a seizure?" I asked dubiously.

She laughed as she sat up. Carefully she stood and took a big step away from where she'd been lying. I could see the outline of her form in the snow, and suddenly I understood what she'd meant.

"You try it," she said, dusting the snow from her legs.

"I don't know," I said. "Looks cold. And wet. How come snow's never wet in the movies? You see people walking with the snow falling around them, sticking to their heads and shoulders, but when they go inside, they're dry, and there're no puddles on the floor..."

Becca laughed again and pushed me, not quite hard enough to make me fall down. Suddenly catching her playful mood, I nudged her back. She shoved me again, and I started to lose my balance. I grabbed her as I tipped, and she landed atop me, face inches from mine.

Now neither of us were laughing. Becca kissed me until my toes started to tingle (or maybe that was from the cold)? Her mouth was hot, her tongue a frenzy of motion. I was almost forgetting where we were when she jumped up and trotted over to stand beneath one of the trees, a twenty-foot pine with sporadic branches for the first six feet from the ground. She curled her mitten-clad fingers at me, beckoning. I struggled to my feet and followed.

"I didn't want you to get too wet there in the snow," she said. "Turn around." I did, and she brushed me off, her hands particularly clingy around my upper thighs. The kissing and rolling around hadn't made just my toes tingly, I had to admit. The moist warmth growing in my cunt was a nice contrast to the clear, cold day.

Becca finished her ministrations and turned me, walking me a step backwards until I was pressed against the tree. "Put your hands up," she said, "and grab hold of that branch above your head." I did, wondering what she had in mind. I felt like a sacrificial virgin. She slipped off her mittens and shoved them in her pocket, then unzipped my down vest.

"Hey!" I protested, reaching down to stop her. She grabbed my hands and pulled them above my head.

"Hold on to the branch," she instructed. "Unless you want me to use that scarf to tie your wrists up there?"

A dull ache spread out from my pussy. We'd talked about trying some light bondage, but hadn't gotten around to it yet, although it intrigued us both. Now, though, wasn't the time I wanted to try. Suddenly I just wanted to do what Becca told me to do.

"Okay, I promise to be good," I whispered. "I'm at your mercy."

Her grin was appreciative and wicked, all at the same time. I knew I was in for it, and boy was I looking forward to it.

"You're crazy, you know that?" I said as she parted my vest and slid her hands beneath my sweater. "What if someone sees us?"

"Nobody ever comes up here," she said. Her hands moved higher, finding my nipples, already budded hard beneath my own silk turtleneck. My body throbbed. "It's private land."

I didn't make another protest, but she added, "I'm just trying to help you live in the moment."

To be honest, I couldn't think much past the maddening feel of her fingers massaging my breasts through the slippery soft silk. She pushed my sweater up and suckled one of my nipples through the silk. When she pulled away, my nips contracted harder, reacting to the cold air and the moisture.

I needed to feel her lips on my flesh, with no fabric barrier between.

Becca knelt before me and tugged the undershirt out of my waistband. My stomach contracted against the rush of air. She nuzzled her cold nose into my belly, and I yelped softly. She laughed, her breath warm against my skin. Goosebumps skittered across my flesh, but I didn't want her to stop.

When she stood to reach my nipples, I saw a flash of white in her hand, and before I could register what it was, she pressed the snow to my breast.

I howled in surprise and nearly let go of the branch. My nipple was so hard it hurt, but a moment later her mouth was on it, hot and sucking hard, and my knees would have buckled if I hadn't been holding on. She repeated the process on my other breast, and again on the first, back and forth, back and forth, until heat and cold became a single burning sensation. I was so close to coming, just from the breast play. My cunt was shivering with tiny spasms that weren't quite orgasms, and the moans coming from my mouth were noises I didn't think I'd ever made before.

"Please…"

Becca pulled my jeans and underwear down below my knees, as far as they'd go before getting caught by the tops of my boots. Frigid air blew across my thighs, but my cunt was still scalding.

"Close your eyes." Becca's voice was thick with lust.

I did what she told me to do. I felt her hand stray between my legs, and using the branch for support, I bent my knees to give her access, since I could spreadn't my entangled feet.

She found that I was wet to my inner thighs. Her caress was too light for me to come, but it held the promise of enduring pleasure. Becca's petiteness extended to her hands, and sometimes, if I was wet enough, she could reach completely inside of me.

I was wet enough now—I was sure of it. But she toyed with my folds, which I imagined were steaming as they came into contact with the winter air.

"Open your mouth."

I expected Becca to bring her hand to my mouth, to slide in her fingers that would be sweet and pungent and slick with my juices.

Instead something hard passed my lips. Hard and cold and long and thick and shaped like...

My eyes flew open. Becca's green eyes had gone nearly black with excitement, but she managed a tremor of a smile as she slid the icicle back out of my mouth. Her other hand was still between my legs, driving most coherent thought from my head.

Still, I knew what she was going to do with that natural, frozen dildo.

My mittened hands clung to the branch above me as she drove it inside of me. It wasn't cold, but burning hot, and oh, so slick, like the glass dildo I'd once owned. I screamed as I clenched and came, bucking my hips as the world whirled in a kaleidoscope of cardinal red and snow white.

I melted.

Andrea Dale

I slid down the trunk, not caring if my down vest tore against the rough bark. Becca dropped to her knees next to me, helped me raise my hips so she could slide my jeans back up so I wasn't sitting bare-assed in the snow.

"You're so freakin' hot," she said, her voice hoarse, "that you completely melted the icicle. Damn."

I couldn't answer. Couldn't speak. My body started to shake from the sobs I couldn't keep down. I wasn't making any noise, but the tears were on my cheeks, and Becca began kissing them off.

"What's wrong, love?" she asked, her voice now tinged with concern.

I managed to form words. "I let go of the branch."

I know she didn't mean to laugh. For what it's worth, I did know she wasn't laughing at me, and I took no offense. Instead I buried my face into her shoulder, glad she wasn't angry.

"Sweetness, what matters is that you trusted me for that long," she said, rocking me back and forth. "You held on a lot longer than I expected. And there was never, ever any penalty for letting go."

*

Christmas Eve. I sat on the floor, my back against the sofa, my head tilted back to watch the psychedelic play of blinking colored lights against the ceiling.

Yes, I was still with Becca, about to celebrate with her one of the biggest, most emotional holidays of the year. Fact was, something had snapped in me, that day in the woods. Or, more rightly put, something had thawed.

I still missed Lindy, and loved her dearly. But she was gone. I had to move on.

Becca had showed me how to trust again.

Before we'd left the clearing that day, Becca had pulled a long, bright red nylon cord out of her pack and wrapped it around the trunk of the tree where we'd just made love. I asked her what she was doing.

"This will tell my dad what tree we want," she said. "He knows where this clearing is; we used to picnic here when I was a kid."

I stared at her, wondering if the lust had fried her brain, too. "But it's twenty feet tall."

Becca led me to the center of the clearing, near the indentations where we'd lain, and put her arms around me. "Look up," she said, and I did. "The top of the tree is perfect," she said.

And she was right: the top of the tree, especially about seven feet or so, was a flawless conical shape, like a storybook Christmas tree.

"We never take the trees from down below," she said. "We always pick a taller one, and then Dad uses the rest of it for firewood." She grinned mischievously, wiggling her body against mine. "Besides, don't you want that reminder sitting in our living room every day for the rest of the month? I think it'll be…quite inspirational."

She'd been right about that, too. Let's just say we'd been creating our own erotic Twelve Days of Christmas.

Now Becca came into the living room, bearing a tray with milk and sugar cookies. She was wearing a Santa hat, with a button pinned to it that displayed a piece of greenery and the words "Mistletoe: Kiss Below".

So I did. For a good long time.

On the Twelfth Day...

Stacie's hands trembled as she untied the green ribbon that bound the Christmas present on her lap. Vince hid his smile, not wanting to distract her. They'd discussed this at length already, but knowing what was in the box—what it represented—was far more powerful than any conversation could ever be.

Just before she opened the box, she looked up at him, eyes seeking reassurance. Now he did smile, and cup her face in his hands. The tree's multicolored lights made ever-changing patterns like stained glass on their skin.

"I love you," he said. Then his smile faded. "Open it."

She shivered at the tone of command in his voice.

"Oh…oh, Vince, it's beautiful," she breathed at her first sight of the red collar nestled in silver tissue paper. She caressed the soft leather, held it up to her throat.

"No." He took it from her hands. She was confused, and he wouldn't hold that against her. "It's mine to put on you," he explained. "You're giving me permission to do that—and to do whatever I want after it's locked around your pretty throat."

Stacie swallowed, but her gaze was steady. "Yes." And as he buckled it on her, she softly sang, "On the first day of Christmas, my true love gave to me…"

*

Twelve days. From Christmas Day through January sixth was the time she gave him to introduce her to BDSM, to guide her into submission, to give her the chance to decide if this was what she wanted for their relationship.

He wanted it. But he loved her too much to give her up if she chose against it.

He loved that she was willing to try.

Day one, the collar. He let her get used to the sensation of wearing it, reminding her of her subservience. In real life, he wouldn't make her wear it all the time, nor would he expect her to wait on him hand and foot. But for this limited time, this learning experience, he sent her off to do the dishes, nudged her chin down if she looked directly at him, reinforced for her his expectations.

On the second day, he spanked her.

They'd played with that a little before, with her squirming and giggling. Now, however, she took it more seriously. When he laid her over his lap and told her not to move, he heard her sharp, indrawn breath.

One for each day, he informed her, and she was to count them off.

"One...sir," she said clearly. "Two, sir. Uh! Three. Three sir!"

Progressively harder, the air reverberating with the crack of his hand against the plump curve of her ass, which steadily reddened.

Dipping a hand between her thighs, he found how wet she was, and the knowledge made him instantly, painfully hard. He took her there on the floor so her tender flesh would rub against the carpet, heightening the sensations.

She sobbed and tensed so hard when she came, he thought she might break apart. But she clutched him, and he told her, unable to keep the pride from his voice, that she'd done very, oh very well.

*

He'd tied her hands with scarves before, so it was a natural progression to add light bondage for the third day. Fur-lined cuffs in a cheerful shade of purple, wrists and ankles. Face-up first, to toy with her nipples and nibble at her pale flesh until she begged—before she realized she wasn't supposed to do that. He was fascinated by the progression of emotions across her face: first shocked realization and guilt, then a level of fear, and then a second realization, not of what she'd done but that she'd be punished for it.

Although she fought to mask it, he definitely saw excitement. Anticipation.

He recuffed her face down with a pillow under her hips and enjoyed her whimpers and squeals as he spanked her, swiftly and soundly.

He slid his cock between her and the pillow and waited while she struggled against the urge to grind her clit against the hard length of him.

When he finally slid into her, it was preceded by the warning not to come until he gave her permission.

He took pity on her and told her to come when he knew she was pitching over the edge anyway. But her writhing against his cock and his hand, her relieved and delighted screams, were all worth it.

*

Clamps adorned her pert breasts on day four. He was so fascinated, so turned on by the sight of the clamps pinching her sensitive nipples, making them pucker and darken, that he kept putting them on and removing them all day.

It was all he could not to pull out a tiny little whip from his locked box and flick it against her imprisoned buds.

No. Not yet. There was time for that later. But from the way she walked when wearing the clips, her chest thrust out just a little, wiggling gently to increase the sensation, he guessed that she might not be averse to stronger stimulation in the future.

That night, he fastened the clamps so the connecting chain would reach her mouth, and he told her not to drop it, no matter what. It made the clips pull deliciously, and didn't allow her to howl her pleasure when he brought her to orgasm with his hands and mouth and cock. Which, he knew, was the hardest thing of all for her.

He pulled the clamps off at the very end, and her final, violent climax drove him over the edge with her.

*

On day five, she grew more nervous. He'd been relatively gentle up until now.

Now, however, he started bringing out the harder stuff.

The spanking bench, which he strapped her to so she couldn't move even if she wanted to disobey him.

The spreader bar, that kept her legs apart and made it harder for her to come. He put a vibrator against her clit and watched her struggle as he stroked his cock. He was heady with need, heady with what he was doing with her and how she was taking it.

So close. So desperate. She would have turned wide blue eyes on him, pleading, if he hadn't blindfolded her.

He'd told her to come at will, but still she fought, the need to bring her legs together to assist her warring with her pitched arousal.

He was so close himself, it was hard to keep his voice steady and stern. "On the count of five," he said. "If you don't come on five, we'll stop, and you'll be punished."

She froze, taking in his words, and then he began. "One… two…"

She came, hard, on five. And so did he.

*

The sixth day was much the same, only with the addition of paddles and a crop to heighten the scenario. Between rounds, he asked for her honest opinion: what she liked, what she didn't like. She had yet to use her safeword, although she'd gasped "yellow" a few times so that he'd ease off.

Still, she slid her fingertips over the welts he'd raised, and her smile spoke volumes.

He didn't overdo it, because he didn't want her too sore for what he'd planned for day seven: New Year's Eve.

She'd been naïve enough to believe that when he told her to wear the panties with the remove-controlled vibrator in them, that they'd be having fun on the way to the club, or on the way home.

Not at the party.

"I'm going to make you come," he said.

"Here—now?" she gasped, and added, just in time, "Sir?"

"Yes. Right here. At this party."

He'd been delighted to discover this was one of her feared fantasies.

"But—"

"If you don't, I'll spank you right here, in front of everyone."

Which would be worse for her? He knew the choice enflamed her. He directed her to the dance floor, thumbed the control. The music pounded; nobody could hear the buzzing. He watched her shudder and cry out, her hips grinding to a beat only she could hear.

"Very good," he said when she returned to him, triumphant and flushed. "Now, for the next one…"

Andrea Dale

*

The butt plug the next day was another test for her, close to but—it turned out—not over her limit. She'd been willing to gently, carefully explore anal play before—just a finger, though, so the toy was another matter altogether. He positioned her on hands and knees, surrounded by well-placed mirrors so she could see the plug sticking out of her nether hole. The swirly green glass contrasted with her blushing skin.

She didn't want to look, but opened her eyes when he ordered her to. Kept them open even as they tried to flutter closed, while he quietly kept up a litany of description: How she looked. How the plug looked. How her ass looked. How hot and slutty she looked.

He didn't tell her that what he'd love to see was one of the plugs that sprouted a horsey tail or peacock feathers. One step at a time. Don't scare her. He kept up the controlled façade, wondering if she had any clue how his emotions raged. He warred between wanting to try everything, wanting to push her to flying ecstasy, and the knowledge that at the end of the twelve days, she might say no and end it all.

He ordered her on top of him, so he could watch in the mirrors.

She carefully took him in, adjusting to the sensation of having both holes stuffed. "Thank you, Sir," she whispered, and he realized why when he found how wet she was.

It boded well for the following day, when he introduced his cock into her ass and watched her flesh pebble with goose bumps as he slowly thrust into her. She didn't come from that alone, but he spent a long time with paddles and vibrators and clamps afterwards, rewarding her deep into the night.

*

Day ten. She was already relaxed and eager, her nipples puckered, when he blindfolded her and cuffed her arms over her head to a convenient hook in the beam.

Most days, he'd told her what her present was to be. Not today.

Today he wanted to catch her off guard.

He paced around her, caressing her as he spoke in soothing but controlling tones. When he had her aroused, pliable, he asked her if she'd do anything for him.

He wasn't surprised when she hesitated. Too soon. But he'd planted the seed. He told her that was okay, that he'd never go against her wishes.

"Anything I suggest, you can ask me to stop anytime. They're just ideas until we implement them."

He grazed her nipples with fingers and teeth before adoring her upturned breasts with clips, the kind with little bells on the ends that chimed when he played with her.

"You like my hands on you, don't you? My mouth, my tongue. My cock." As he spoke the last, he rubbed the head of his penis against her slickness, along the hard bud of her clit.

She trembled in her bonds, the muscles in her arms tight as she clenched her fists. "Yes," she repeated in breathy little gasps. "Oh. Yes. Yes. Sir."

In a quick, careful motion, he replaced his cock with a dildo. One stroke with his cock, then one with the dildo, so she couldn't quite tell. He slipped the dildo into her pussy, gently fucking her with it, not enough pressure or speed to bring her to orgasm.

He did the same with a smaller one, well-lubed, slipping it into her ass while he told her how good he felt there. She whimpered and agreed, far gone enough not to tell the difference.

Back and forth. One, then the other. Toying with the dildos, and the clamps on her breasts. She was disoriented, but in a good way, flying on the myriad of stimulation.

He lifted her—she was such a slight thing—and eased her onto his cock, her legs wrapped around his waist. Like last night, her pussy was so tight, the slim dildo in her ass pressing against the length of him.

She gave him so much. He didn't even feel the urge to drive into her, knowing he had to move carefully.

"How would it feel," he asked, his voice rough with passion, "to have *two* sets of hands on you? *Two* mouths, *two* cocks? *Two* men worshipping your body, inside you, all over you?"

"I…think…" She took a deep breath. "I think I would… like that, sir."

"How do you know it's not happening right now?" he asked.

Time stopped. He felt her entire body go taut as her mind raced to assimilate the possibility. Even her orgasm seemed to go in slow motion. He was aware of it building inside her, gearing up like a tidal wave gathering strength and racing towards the shore.

When it crested, her convulsions sent him tumbling into the surf along with her.

*

He pushed her limits again the next day, along with again throwing her off guard, letting her believe things were happening that actually weren't. Perception was everything. The sight of the needle, long and slender, before he blindfolded her. The judicious words he chose, describing how beautiful she'd look with her nipples pierced. The careful application of an ice cube on her breast followed by the touch of a needle—never breaking the skin—but she didn't know that.

She knew only ecstasy.

*

Epiphany.

The sixth of January dawned glitteringly clear. Vince brought Stacie breakfast in bed, the French roast steaming, a single peach rose in a vase.

She was understandably confused, but at his urging she enjoyed the mushroom-and-asagio omelet, the fresh fruit and croissant. He nibbled off her plate, having already eaten while he prepared the food.

When she was finished, she looked at him expectantly for the collar.

He shook his head, not even looking to where it sat on the night table. "For twelve days, I promised you gifts," he said. "And for twelve days, you promised to accept them."

She put her hand to her throat. "Have I not…?"

"No," he said quickly, taking both her hands in his. "You've been amazing. Perfect."

He took a deep breath. "Our agreement was twelve days. On this, the twelfth day, this is the gift I give you: Me. Everything I've shown you, everywhere I've tried to take you. Understand this—I will always love you, always be with you, no matter what you decide, no matter if you decide that what we've explored isn't how you want to be.

"But I'm always here for you, and that's all I can give you, in whatever way you'll have me."

Her answer was simple. A sweet, dazzling smile, before she bowed her head and held out the collar to him.

Let It Snow

Christmas morning.

I sighed a slowly waking sigh and rolled over, my hand reaching out instinctively to brush against Martin's hip. When I encountered nothing, I woke up a little more, remembering.

I respected him so much for taking on graveyard shift at the hospital so other doctors—especially those with kids—could be home on Christmas morning. But it was still strange not to have him there with me.

Just as it was strange that I'd have no snow for Christmas.

I squinted at the clock. Martin would be home in less than an hour. We'd opened stockings last night, before he'd left for work, and even had time for another celebration that involved me wearing festive, holly-dotted stockings. My core clenched at the delicious memory, and I smiled into the pillow.

Martin's volunteering to take the graveyard shift showed true holiday spirit, and I'd have him home soon, to celebrate the day. But it also meant we hadn't been able to travel back east to see my family for the holidays.

It meant that I wouldn't have snow.

Martin was a southern California boy, born and bred. He'd tease me: "If we want snow, we go up in the mountains to visit it." And I'd reply: "You don't *travel* to weather!"

And so I'd put on a good face, a positive attitude, all season. It wasn't easy, though. I was used to skiing—both down-hill and cross-country—the day after Christmas; used to watching big fat flakes drift down outside the window as we opened presents that morning; used to trudging up the long driveway to collect the newspaper in the silent, untouched hush of pre-dawn, new-fallen snow.

This year, walking through the Santa Monica Promenade, the holiday music blaring and the light poles wrapped with faux fir trim, I thought I was on a movie set. I couldn't understand that it was winter, what with the sun glinting off the ocean a few blocks away.

Oh, at least we'd had some grey, gloomy days and fog— and it looked like today would be one of those—but still…

Martin promised we'd go up to Big Bear a few days after Christmas, but it just wasn't the same.

No, I wouldn't let Martin know that sometime tears pricked my eyes, that sometimes I even let a few of those tears loose, and then a few more when the air wasn't cold enough to freeze them to my cheeks.

Christmas morning. Not a time for mourning. I threw back the covers and headed for the shower.

I had the egg casserole in the oven and was about to toss on the bacon when Martin got home.

He kissed me 'til I was breathless, then said, "I've got a surprise for you."

When I saw he had our waterproof motorcycle gear out, I assumed we were going for a ride. Maybe to Big Bear, starting our trip early? Wouldn't it make more sense to take the car? Or maybe we were going down to the beach for a romantic picnic….

I wasn't prepared for what I saw when he flung open the back door.

The ground was white.

In movies, they use soap flakes for snow. That was my first thought. But this didn't smell like soap. It smelled like *snow*.

I hadn't put my gloves on yet. I knelt down and scooped up a handful. Cold. Wet.

I stared at Martin, who couldn't contain his grin.

"Aaron," he said. "When he was a kid, his friend's dad and uncle drove up into the mountains one Christmas morning and dumped a truckload of snow in their front yard. Aaron said his friend was the most popular kid on the street—until it all melted that afternoon." He planted a kiss on my forehead. "Aaron, being Jewish, didn't mind doing me a favor this morning."

I tried to speak, but I just couldn't.

Martin threw an arm out to indicate our snow-laden back yard. "So, show me what's so amazing about snow."

His gesture brought me to tears, and even though I logically knew that if this were really winter, the tears would be freezing to my lashes, I didn't care. He'd brought me *snow for Christmas*.

I hauled him in for a proper kiss. I put my hands on his face and he did the same, cradling my jaw in that intimate gesture that takes my breath away. I don't know if he'd been playing in the snow already, but his hands were cold against my skin.

But the kiss…the kiss sizzled.

Last night I'd worn sexy stockings dotted with holly and we'd had a good romp, but this kiss took things to another level, one I hadn't felt since those first heady dates. Love and lust intertwined like stripes on a candy cane, and I felt it all the way down to the pit of my belly, to my groin now heavy with need.

I dragged my lips from his. He sucked in a deep breath, his dark brown eyes all pupil and *want*.

"I just want to drag you into the house and have my way with you," I admitted, fighting through desire to speak. "But snow first—before it melts. You want what's amazing about snow?" I cleared my throat. "Well," I said, "for starters, snowmen."

The snow wasn't quite the right consistency, but we made a heroic attempt at a little snow dude, all the while joking about the *Calvin & Hobbes* comic strips where Calvin makes zombie snowmen or snowmen who look like they've been run over by his dad's car. And, yes, there was kissing in between, moments where time stopped and it was just *us*. Our motorcycle gear was a barrier to caresses, and somehow that made everything hotter, harkening back to the days of necking in the car, the fever-pitch of excitement and frustration of never quite touching where you wanted to touch or where you needed to be touched.

For example, when we made snow angels. It's a good thing we have a big, private back yard, because Martin's first attempts left something to be desired. I showed him how, and he tried to copy me, but…no. Just, no.

Finally I threw my hands up and said, "Okay, come here." I lay down in a patch of still-pristine snow, warning him not to step into the boundaries my body would make. "Lie down on top of me," I said, "limb to limb. Don't disturb the snow around me."

Admittedly, that wasn't easy, but I managed to shift my arms and legs to give him places to touch the ground before he could settle flat atop me.

Oh. My. Maybe this wasn't the best idea.

My plan had been to create a snow angel so he could feel how it was done—kind of like when a kid stands on her dad's feet to learn dance moves.

This was…much more intimate.

His fingers were threaded through mine, his chest pressed to mine, his groin against mine, and through the layers of ballistic gear I could feel his erection hard against my pubic bone.

I'd have to wash my own gear afterwards; I knew that already. I was hot and slick inside my pants, the layer of comfy, moisture-wicking leggings not doing much of a wicking job.

His face hovered right about mine, his breath warm and smelling like the candy cane he'd nibbled on before he left work.

"Hm," he said with an experimental thrust of his hips that made me catch my breath. "I'm beginning to see what's so fun about snow."

It was one of those deciding moments. I wanted him, badly—oh yes, yes I did.

But…*snow!*

I spread my legs, keenly aware of the sexual nature of the movement, the childhood innocence swept away. Open. Wanting.

His legs moved with me, and his arms with mine as I drew them down to my sides and back up again, then repeating the motion with both our arms and legs.

"And that," I whispered against his mouth, "is how you make a snow angel. But the trick—the trick is to get up without fucking it up."

Following my instructions, he got to his feet without marring the angel we'd created, then held out his hand to me. The loss of his body weight against me left me keenly bereft. I let him help me to my feet, hopping away from the bottom of the angel.

Hand in hand, we viewed our creation.

And then I stuffed the handful of snow I'd grabbed before I stood right down the back of his neck.

What resulted was a full-on, giggling, return-to-childhood snowball fight. Martin may not have grown up in snow, but he figured the concept out pretty quickly, and he's damned competitive. As am I.

The snow wasn't especially sticky, but it did its job, and soon the parts of us that were exposed were wet and cold. (As compared to the parts of me that were still wet and hot.)

There wasn't a lot of snow left; it hadn't been thick on the ground, and we'd scooped up a fair amount of it. We simultaneously flung a truly pathetic excuse for a snowball at each other and, without speaking, called a truce by meeting halfway for a kiss.

Thankfully our backyard has high fences. Martin backed me up against one of them, unzipping my jacket and stripping it off of me as we went. The shirt I had on underneath had a built-in shelf bra, so when he shoved it up, there was nothing to hinder his hands against my breasts.

His very cold hands.

But the juxtaposition of cold nipples and hot cunt was thrilling. My nipples were so hard, they hurt, in a painfully erotic way, by the time he bent to take one in his warm mouth.

I didn't get his jacket off, but once it was unzipped I was able to slide my hands up under his shirt, find his small, flat nipples, tickle them the way I know makes him wild with need.

His hips bucked against mine when my icy fingertips found those sensitive nubs.

It was time to go inside.

We shed clothes as we went, and made it as far as the living room, where I'd lit the gas fire in anticipation of Martin's arrival. He pushed me back onto the sofa, lifted my hips with his hands under my ass, and discovered just how wet I'd gotten.

His face wasn't cold against my thighs—despite the snow, the air simply wasn't that chilly—but my brain insisted it must be, because we'd been out in the snow. Somehow, that made the warmth of his tongue feel hotter.

Hot and cold. Ice and fire. Snow where there shouldn't be, except by the power of love.

I was on the edge, but I wanted Martin inside of me, so I squirmed out from under him and turned to kneel on the couch, ass thrust out and inviting. He didn't need a greater hint.

His cock—hot, rigid, and glorious—sank into me, and I reached down to feel the place where our bodies met, feel my lips stretch around his hardness, before I stroked my clit in time to his thrusts, and came, and came again when he did.

"Merry Christmas," he murmured it my ear, and then something about playing with ice cubes later.

*

Afterwards I stood, wrapped in a rose-print cotton robe, cradling a cup of hot cocoa laced with crème de menthe, watching patches of green grow larger on the lawn as the snow melted away. The egg casserole was a loss, but Martin was frying bacon and scrambling eggs. The English muffins would pop out of the toaster in a minute or two.

After breakfast, he'd take a nap, and then we'd head to his sister's place for a present exchange and early Christmas dinner. He had two more mid shifts, and then we'd head up to Big Bear, and real snow.

The melting snow outside felt pretty real to me, though.

As real as our love.

Santa Claus is Comin'

*A*re you naughty or nice, little girl?

"Naughty" was the answer Jessica always came down on. Naughty, because she had a naughty, perverse, filthy little secret.

It had all started when she was a child, believing in magic and wonder and Santa Claus. The very first time she saw the Rankin-Bass special "Santa Claus is Comin' to Town," she'd been swept away. The woman in the animation was also named Jessica, so it was a short leap (just a hop and a skip, really) from there to little-girl Jessica imagining and pretending *she* was that Jessica.

Good, virtuous, animated Jessica helped rescue Kris Kringle so that he could bring toys to the children of Sombertown. She went on to marry him and become Mrs. Claus. And like little-girl Jessica, she yearned for a pretty porcelain doll to call her own.

When little-girl Jessica became young-adult Jessica, with all the attendant hormone overload, it had then been a short tumble into the gutter to imagining what Jessica and Kris did on their wedding night.

In specific, kinky detail.

Kris had this wide-eyed, pink-cheeked innocence to him, and that made the fantasies all the more depraved.

Now it was Christmas Eve once again, and Jessica had been sipping eggnog and wrapping presents and singing along with the animated special. (Oh, how she'd celebrated the day it was finally released on DVD!)

When Winter gave Kris the magic snow globe that allowed him to see who'd been naughty or nice, she shivered as she always did. Her clit pulsed even as her cheeks flushed. Naughty, always naughty.

Technically, Kris was quite the bad boy himself. He insisted on standing up to the Burgermeister Meisterburger and bringing toys to Sombertown when they were outlawed.

Jessica went for the bad boys, the rebels. Especially if they were redheads.

She set the final wrapped present under the tree, knocked back the last of the eggnog, and turned off all the lights except for the multicolored ones that blinked on the tree. Then she went to the bedroom to prepare for her final Christmas Eve ritual.

She shimmied into a scarlet satin peek-a-boo bra with the nipples cut out and matching crotchless panties, a short red velvet skirt trimmed with white faux fur, and thigh-high stockings striped red-and-white like candy canes. Jessica in the cartoon was always primly attired, but Jessica in real life knew about dressing for sex.

Adjusting the red-and-white velvet hat on her head, she settled back down on the living room sofa and closed her eyes.

"Naughty Jessica."

In her fantasies, he looked the same as he did in the animation: impossibly smooth skin, unusually large blue eyes, unearthly cartoon features. His motions weren't quite as smooth as they should be, but his shoulders were as broad as in the cartoon, something little kids probably never noticed.

"I *am* naughty," she purred, running her hands across her bare torso and over her bra. Her nipples had sprung to attention at his words, begging for his touch. "What are you going to do about it? Put coal in my stocking?"

His gaze dropped to her legs, his expression so shockingly lascivious that if he'd looked that way in the Rankin-Bass special, mothers everywhere would have been horrified—or gotten impossibly wet, just like Jessica was doing now.

"Seems to me," he said, "that your stocking are well filled. Guess I'll have to find some other way to punish you."

Jessica moaned, a fresh wave of desire pulsing through her.

He sat on a throne-like chair that had appeared in her living room like magic, just as he had. (Well, he'd come down the chimney, right? Like *that* wasn't phallic.) He patted his thighs. "Sit on Santa's lap."

On legs gone wobbly with lust, she obeyed. He drew her in for a bruising kiss, nipping at her lower lip until she gasped. Tweaking her nipples with his fingers, pinching hard enough to poise on the edge of pain, he said "What do you want for Christmas, hm?"

"You," Jessica managed, squirming on his lap. Beneath his red trousers, she felt his erection, and she wanted his cock inside her.

She knew she'd have to wait for the privilege, but it didn't stop her from asking.

"Well, let's see what Santa has in his sack for you." He picked up the bulging bag and began pulling out toys.

Her breath caught. Every year they were different. Maybe butt plugs and whips; maybe rabbit-fur mittens and tickly feathers.

This time he had clamps for her nipples, ones that ended with little green holiday bells. He always seemed to know how to accessorize the outfit she chose each year. She hissed against the pain as the teeth nipped into her sensitive flesh, and her cheeks flushed hot as the bells jingled merrily.

Red and gold ribbon, the kind you'd use to wrap a package, now wound between and over her wrists. He tied them together in a jaunty bow. Then he picked her up (this was magic and fantasy, after all) and arranged her over his lap, head down, ass up, his erection digging into her stomach.

He tugged her panties down just below the curve of her bottom, stripped off his gloves.

When she clenched her cheeks, he reached down and tugged on those vicious clamps, and she squealed.

"Hush now," he said. "Not a creature was stirring, not even a mouse."

She pressed her lips together and made no more sound than a whimper as he blistered her butt with his hand. Rosy cheeks, all part of the Santa milieu, but this wasn't what most people thought of. When his hand connected with her ass, it stung; when he paused, it throbbed. Throbbed in the same way her tortured nipples throbbed, throbbed in time with her wanting clit, her empty cunt.

One year he'd shown up with Topper the penguin, who'd stared at her with unblinking black eyes. Another year the Winter Warlock joined him, the two of them pushing her to her limits and beyond. Still, Kris was the only one she wanted. The only one she needed, craved.

He nudged her off his lap and stood. "Suck my cock," he said.

Dropping to her knees, Jessica unbuckled his wide shiny black belt and tugged town his red trousers. He sat back, sighing as she wrapped her still-bound hands around him.

His flesh felt smoother than a normal man's, cooler, unwrinkled. More like a dildo than a real penis. (She'd never seen him flaccid, so she didn't know how exactly that worked.) Under her hands and wet mouth, though, it grew warm, and a hard cock would feel incredible inside her no matter what it was made of.

She was already wet from the clamps and the spanking, even as she shifted from the discomfort of her heels rubbing into her stinging skin as she knelt before him. She would have loved to touch herself, release the ache between her thighs, but for now she concentrated on him, giving him the best head she could.

One year he'd given her a vibrator, watched her as he gave her instructions, making her come again and again until she thought she was too sensitive, then forcing her to come yet again.

Another year he'd fitted her with a bit and a butt plug with a brown-and-white tuft of a tail. He'd bent her over the arm of the throne, tugged on reins as he pounded into her, calling out the names of his reindeer.

Now, he finally helped her to her feet and led her to the sofa. Sitting down, he guided her onto his lap to straddle him. The scratchy wool of his half-pulled-down pants was like sandpaper on her ass when she sank all the way down on him.

The bells jingled merrily as she posted up and down on that smooth hard cock. Then she was grinding back and forth, only his hands on her waist keeping her from toppling off as she shuddered and moaned through her climax.

His own shout was jolly, the ho-ho-hos jerking from him in time to his final orgasmic thrusts.

*

Jessica awoke with a start, her neck aching from her uncomfortable splay on the sofa. In the blinking light, she saw that the cookies and eggnog she'd left out were gone.

Her inner thighs were sticky with pungent come, her ass tender and hot.

There was a new present under the tree, a box wrapped in blue paper with silver snowflakes printed on it, topped with a big silver bow. Jessica held with the tradition of opening one present on Christmas Eve, and that present was always the one from him.

With a tender smile, she lifted the porcelain doll from the box. She'd leave it under the tree for now; later, she'd put it into the case with all the others.

She unplugged the lights on the tree and headed upstairs to bed, weary and sated and already yearning for next Christmas Eve.

It wasn't sugarplums she'd be dreaming of…

Mrs. Claus and the Naughty Elf

It was hard for Mrs. Claus to be merry on Christmas Eve when a year ago, Mr. Claus had run off with the Peppermint Stick girl.

Samantha Burgess peered over her half-circle glasses at the line of children winding out of the grotto, keeping a jolly smile pasted on her face even as inside she felt as cold as the winter wind. For twenty-three years, she and Mac had been Mr. and Mrs. Claus at North Pole Village, until he'd run off with that skinny bimbo in a striped spandex bodystocking that made her look like a barbershop pole.

Which explained why Mac hadn't found it funny when Samantha had compared the Peppermint Stick girl to a barbershop pole.

Samantha amused herself with the mental picture of shoving a barbershop pole up Mac's...

"Hey, Mrs. Claus."

"Hey, Elf Boy." She grinned at Jeremy—who was shaking snow off his holly-green elf hat—and ushered a little girl, eyes wide and glowing at the prospect of meeting *the* Santa, towards the big wooden chair where Mac's replacement sat, belly shaking like a bowl full of jelly.

Jeremy no longer looked quite as elf-like as he had when he'd started working at North Pole Village on his winter break when he was a scrawny high school junior. Since then, he'd grown more than a few inches, and filled out proportionally, too. But his lanky face could still split into a boyish grin that no doubt charmed the ladies, and his dark hair flopped onto his forehead just like a character in one of those Rankin-Bass holiday specials.

Egads—he was in grad school now. Samantha refused to do the math. It would just make her feel even older.

Jeremy took over for the exhausted elf who'd been assisting her. On light days, they had just a couple of elves to take tickets and generally help out. During frantic times like tonight, they had several, with multiple shifts—fixing the fake snow covering when it got rumpled, helping parents find the bathrooms, drying the tears of hysterical children. The latest Peppermint Stick girl—who'd refused to wear spandex, bless her heart—stood on the far side of Santa, giving each child a candy cane after he or she hopped off the Big Guy's lap, content in the knowledge that he'd bring exactly what he'd been instructed to on Christmas morning.

"How're you holding up, Mrs. C?" Jeremy asked.

"Tougher than a decades-old fruitcake."

Her girlfriends had all been sympathetically horrified by Mac's defection. Samantha had allowed herself a few months of wallowing in grief, followed by a brisk selling of the house and ritual burning of all the clothes he'd left behind, along with his Bon Jovi concert memorabilia. Then she'd gotten on with her life. She'd even helped interview for the new Mr. Claus.

Her girlfriends had supported, applauded, bolstered. But come the holiday season, they'd pretty much vanished into their own worlds, focusing on celebrating the season with their loved ones. Jeremy was one of the few people who'd remembered just how difficult the season might be for Samantha.

He was a good kid. Nice parents, too. They'd raised him well.

"I know you said you'll be with your brother's family tomorrow," he said. "But do you have plans for tonight? If not, how about going out for hot chocolate after?"

She cocked her head. "You know, I'd like that. You're sure you don't have other plans?"

"Nope. Heading to my folks' in the morning."

By the end of the evening, she was ready for something a lot stronger than hot chocolate. Christmas Eve was always mayhem at North Pole Village, and this year had been no exception. Kids everywhere, running in circles because they were so hyped up on anticipation and massive amounts of sugar. One got so excited that he peed on the new Santa, and Samantha had to take over in the big chair for a few rounds while he went and changed into his backup suit.

Finally, it was over. The final child had been booted out the door, the stereo system had finally been turned off before they heard another repeat of "Do They Know It's Christmas?" and Samantha had another 1980s nostalgia moment.

When Samantha came out of the women's changing room, Jeremy's jaw dropped.

"Woah, Mrs. C!"

"What?" She looked down at herself. Had she put her sweater on inside-out?

"You…you look fantastic."

Something in Jeremy's voice made her peer at him. She saw him swallow.

"I, uh, guess I haven't seen you out of costume this year," he managed.

And then she understood. She'd lost thirty pounds since Mac left. She wasn't anywhere close to the barbershop-pole girl's frame, but she was pleased that the marriage weight that had crept up on her over the years was gone. The elliptical machine had borne much of the brunt of her anger, and she figured exercising had benefited her mental health as well as her physical.

Yes, last year she wouldn't have been wearing black leggings, a hip-skimming skinny black sweater with a sprinkling of holly at the neckline, and knee-high black leather boots.

This year, they'd had to pad her costume.

The look she saw in Jeremy's eyes scared her a little. She grabbed her long wool winter coat and threw it on.

"I'm buying the first round," she said, and headed for the door.

*

The first round of hot chocolate—complete with mini-marshmallows and whipped cream *and* chocolate sprinkles—in hand, they settled into a creaking leather booth at the twenty-four-hour diner. Outside, snowflakes glittered and danced in the streetlight's aura.

She found herself telling Jeremy about the barbershop pole comment, and he grinned. "I always loved your sense of humor, Mrs. C.," he said. "Personally, I thought of her as Mr. C.'s 'ho ho whore.'"

It was Samantha's turn to howl, putting her head down on the table when she could barely breathe from the laughter.

When she pulled herself together and dabbed at her streaming eyes, Jeremy patted her hand.

"I was worried about you," he admitted. "You didn't deserve being treated like shit. I'm really happy you've kept your sense of humor."

"If I didn't laugh, I'd cry," she said, knowing it was a lame joke, but her brain was failing her. Jeremy's hand had stopped patting, and now curved over hers, warm and comforting, and...

He was young enough to be her son.

He was old enough to make his own choices.

His eyes were dark, all pupil, not from drugs, but, she guessed, adrenaline. No, be honest, it wasn't adrenaline. What poured off him in waves was not adrenaline.

Samantha hadn't had sex—at least, not with anything other than her trusty vibrator collection—since Mac. She hadn't entirely wanted to. She'd thought, maybe, that things had just sort of frozen down south.

The mere touch of Jeremy's hand on hers was causing a sudden thaw.

"I'm probably overstepping my bounds here," Jeremy said, "but do you know just how sexy you are? You're confident enough to make jokes…yeah, that's really sexy."

She groped for something to say. "I'm old enough to be your mother."

Jeremy regarded her solemnly. Without taking his eyes off hers, he drew her hand to his mouth and kissed her palm, with just the barest hint of tongue tickling the sensitive flesh.

She felt it all the way through her body.

"And I'm old enough to not care," he said.

*

After the divorce she'd bought a small Craftsman bungalow, one story, with a gabled roof and exposed wood inside that hadn't been painted over. It glowed richly in the sparkling white lights of the tree she'd set up in the corner. Samantha lit candles on the mantle and around the room, in colors that matched the tree decorations: burgundy, forest green, antique gold.

The flames flickered over Jeremy's face, highlighting his cheekbones and reflecting in the darkness of his eyes.

Samantha found the gold-etched cordial glasses and the crème de menthe. "The hot chocolate was missing something," she said.

He took the glass and raised it in toast. "To Christmas Eve," he said. "Nothing more, nothing less."

She toasted, drank, and let him draw the sweater over her head and the leggings down her legs.

She'd lost weight, yes, but also come to terms with what a forty-plus body had to offer: more pillowy breasts, more rounded hips. Any fleeting concern she had vanished when she remembered that Jeremy's last girlfriend, whom he'd dated for several years in college, had been adorably plump. He didn't seem to want a barbershop pole.

He clinched that when his eyes darkened at the sight of her, mostly naked in the low lights. He reached out and ran his hand down her side, skimming the red silk camisole and matching boy shorts.

"People have no idea what Mrs. Claus is hiding under her suit," he said. "If only they knew. Every father in town would be bringing his kids. Every other guy would borrow children to bring."

"You sound rather smug," Samantha said.

"Are you kidding?" He grinned at her. "The poor slobs have no idea what they're missing. *I'm* the one that gets to sit on Mrs. Claus's sexy lap."

Enough with the talking. She stepped forward and kissed him.

The thawing down south resembled melting ice in the hot spring sun: dripping. She'd almost forgotten just how good a good kiss could be. She briefly wondered if every married couple lost that element of sex, then allowed herself to forget. Forget Mac, forget the barbershop pole, forget everything except the tongue probing her mouth and the strong male hands caressing her body, cupping her ass and pulling her forward until she felt the hard length of his cock pressing against her belly.

It had been so long since she'd had someone new, someone different, and her body burned in ways she'd forgotten it could. That hint of nerves in the gut, that curiosity. Exploring kisses. Inquisitive hands.

Oh *yes*. She wriggled against him, rubbing her silk-covered nipples against his chest. He got the hint and pulled back just enough to slide his hands between them and find her breasts.

"More," she whispered when he skimmed her with his palms. "Harder."

"That's good," he murmured. "Tell me what you want, tell me what you like." He punctuated his words with pinches, first gentle and then getting harder as she moaned with pleasure.

"I like it when you twist them," she said, even as the honest confession, along with his compliance, made her gasp. "You can bite, too."

"I like a woman who's secure enough to call the shots," Jeremy said. "A lot of girls aren't."

She hadn't always been. But she'd learned. Another benefit, she realized through the passion-haze, of age and experience.

Despite his request for guidance, Jeremy was obviously no novice. A bit clumsy, perhaps, or maybe it was just excitement that made his hands tremble. But damn if he didn't know his way around her body, tweaking her nipples, bending his head to suckle them and then blow warm breath across them, making them bead even harder.

Her knees buckled under the erotic onslaught, and she stepped backwards, pulling him with her down onto the sofa.

He paused long enough to strip his sweater off over his head, revealing a smooth, lean chest, and peel off his jeans. Samantha boldly checked out his crotch. His high-cut navy briefs were losing the battle to contain his cock; the smooth head pressed against the elastic band.

He saw her watching and grinned, thrusting his hips forward and posing. She reached out for him, but he scooted backwards and dropped to his knees.

"You first," he said.

She felt her inner walls flutter and clench at his words. There was nothing like lying back and being worshipped, and if he was offering, she was going to accept it gladly.

He nipped at her hip, scraped his fingers along her inner thigh, and she shivered. Rough but respectful, aware.

Another brief flash of insecurity. What if it took her too long to—?

But his tongue snaked between her folds, lapping at her juices, and then he moved up to her clit and settled in as if enjoying a feast. She tugged at her own nipples as the heaviness built in her belly, in her cunt.

She tensed, a subtle movement, but he caught it. He picked up the pace, flicking his tongue faster over the hard nub, but at the same time backing off on the pressure, just a little, as she became more sensitive.

The familiar roll started, a wave building, growing, curling…

The wave broke, and she screamed as she drowned in it.

And then, *oh god oh god*, he didn't stop, and the undertow caught her and tossed her and flung her into another orgasm, sharper and stronger than the first.

When she came back to reality, he was fishing in the pocket of his jeans. It took her a moment to realize what he was looking for—it had been a long time since she'd had to worry about condoms.

"Let me," she offered, taking the tiny package from him. A wet spot shimmered, spreading, on his strained briefs. She slid them down his hips, and his cock popped out, long and slender like the rest of him, but far from skinny. She ran the tip of her finger through the precome, licked it off. His eyes were half-closed, intent, as he watched her.

Tossing the packet away, she slid the condom onto the head of his cock, then used her lips to roll it the rest of the way down. His hips jerked convulsively, and when she reached up to wrap her hand around him, he gently pulled her arm away.

"You do that, we're all done, at least for a while."

She understood. As tempting as it was to revisit just how quickly a young man could bounce back, she was still quivering from the aftershocks of two amazing orgasms, and she wanted him inside her. She doubted he'd protest too much.

She stood and nudged him down onto the sofa. Straddling his thighs, she braced herself against the back of the sofa and sank down onto his long, hard length.

Bliss. She paused, exulting in the feel of a cock deep inside her again.

His head was back, his eyes closed and his lip caught between his teeth. She clenched her inner muscles, and heard his sharply indrawn breath.

No sense in teasing either of them any longer. The elliptical machine had provided an added benefit that she hadn't realized until now—her thighs, as come-weak as they were, didn't protest when she posted up over him, when she gave a little shimmy of her hips after she slid back down.

Another orgasm raced down her spine, shook her body, and as she tumbled out the other side of it, Jeremy grabbed her hips and thrust up into her, once, twice, three times in rapid succession, or maybe it was more than that. But she saw his face twist, heard his hoarse cry, and felt her body shiver, just enough, in answer.

*

Her camisole was bunched up under her arms; her panties were hanging off the antlers of a woven willow reindeer near the tree. Her hair, she knew, was wild.

She'd never felt so wanton and sexy and alive.

Jeremy returned from the bathroom and saw her. "Wow," he said, kneeling by the sofa and cupping her breast. "I wish I could stay here all night."

She patted his hand. "I need my beauty sleep," she said. "And you need to get home."

As he tugged on his jeans and sweater, she ditched the cami top and tucked the chenille throw from the sofa around her body. Then she walked him to the door and kissed him goodbye. That would be the end of it, of course; she wouldn't see him until next season at North Pole Village. With his talents, he'd surely have another lucky girlfriend in hand. And she was fine with that.

"Merry Christmas, Mrs. Claus." He winked, then bounded down the steps to his car.

She stood in the doorway, watching the snowflakes dance in the porch light.

She cocked her head. If she listened very, very hard, she was sure she could hear the sound of bells jingling.

Chuckling, she closed the door. She didn't need Santa to make her Christmas merry.

Teresa Noelle Roberts

၄

Christmas Blizzard

"Another cancellation," I sighed as I hung up the phone. "Merry fucking Christmas to you too!"

The promise of a "blizzard of the new century" threatening to rival the infamous, deadly Blizzard of '78, here on the far tip of Cape Cod where snow rarely sticks at all, had cleared the few winter tourists out of Provincetown long before the snow actually hit. I'm sure some of the locals were pleased, but it was making for a less than happy day at our bed-and-breakfast. We'd been booked full for tonight, Christmas Eve—women who'd decided on a romantic day in P'town and either breakfast in bed or a big pajama-clad family-style breakfast on Christmas morning—but one by one, they'd been canceling. The couple who'd just called had been our last hold-outs; they'd gotten as far as Providence, Rhode Island on their way from New York City, creeping through a near whiteout, and had decided to hole up in a hotel there for the day instead of risking the rest of the drive.

Lucie circled her arms around me from behind. "Look on the bright side. We have Christmas to ourselves! When was the last time we got to spend a day, any day, without an inn full of guests? And we can enjoy the inn all decorated and pretty instead of hiding up in our little cave." Her hands slid up from my waist to cup my breasts. "What's the point of owning a lesbian romantic haven if we can't enjoy it ourselves sometimes?"

Good point, I thought, as her small, hard hands sent waves of sensation radiating out from my breasts. Our apartment above the garage was the only part of the property we hadn't succeeded in making luxurious, the only part we hadn't bothered decorating for Christmas/Solstice/generic midwinter cheer. But left alone, nothing would stop us from enjoying all the amenities we offered to guests. "Let's start in the Lavender Room," I whispered. "I'd gotten it all ready for the folks who just called."

We all but ran there. We'd had a fire going against the window-rattling gale, and the room was toasty warm, the flames casting interesting shadows on the lavender walls. We shared a quiet moment enjoying the sensation of pretending to be guests, appreciating the beautiful color scheme we'd chosen, the richness of plump pillows, velvet duvet cover, brocaded drapes. The room smelled delicious, like Christmas cookies (we'd gone crazy baking for the guests and would now be eating gingerbread women and pfeffernüsse for weeks), wood smoke, pine, and, of course, lavender. Yeah, our guests had it pretty good—and today, so did we.

Then clothes began flying everywhere. Soon we were naked and lying in each other's arms on the Oriental rug in front of the fire.

Just long, languid kisses at first, and pressing together, loving how our breasts brushed against each other, how our legs intertwined to allow maximum skin contact. The warmth transmuted into heat and the heat filled me, igniting nipple and clit and pussy and every inch of skin in between. From her movements against me, I could tell Lucie was in the same place. It had been a long time since we'd taken the time to just make out like this.

Finally I pulled away, sat up. Lucie's skin glimmered with a fine sheen of sweat. Her nipples were hard, crinkled with excitement and moisture gleamed between her parted legs. "Beautiful," I breathed. I moved to touch her, but she shook her head. "The floor's hard, and I've always loved that sleigh bed."

If I could have picked her up and carried her, I would have. It seemed appropriate in that room with its Victorian aura. Alas for that fantasy. Lucie, while shorter than I am, does chimney work in fall and winter and landscaping in summer, and she's dense with muscle. So I just gave her a hand up instead and whirled her over to the bed.

It was high and puffy and enveloping and her café-au-lait skin—Lucie is an interesting ethnic mix that includes Cape Verdean, French-Canadian, and Mohawk—looked both darker and creamier against the purple velvet duvet. I dove onto the bed next to her, squealing "Whee!" and for a minute all we could do was giggle. Then I began to stroke her and the giggles faded into sighs.

Silken skin over firm muscles, and small breasts with prominent, plum-colored nipples, and the tight, black curls that drew my eye to her pussy, just as plum-dark as her nipples and currently juicier than any plum I'd ever encountered—I stroked and kissed my way down Lucie's body to that spot and began to lick.

I've given a lot of thought to what Lucie actually tastes like. The briny sweetness of oysters—Wellfleet oysters, eaten in Wellfleet just hours after they were harvested—always come to mind, but there's a hint of smoke and spice there too, and a fragrance that adds to the mystery. Lucie tastes like Lucie, I suppose, and she's delicious.

She filled my mouth, my nostrils, all my senses. In turn I filled her with two fingers, crooking them to tantalize that sensitive little node that someone unpoetically named the G-spot. Slick and smooth and gripping, she rode my hand and mouth, cooing and mewling to herself. Strangely lady-like noises, as if she was afraid of being overheard. But that was just Lucie's way. At other times, she's outspoken, with the hearty voice of someone who works outdoors a lot. In bed, she becomes deceptively quiet. (For the first year we were together, I tried everything I could think of to make her scream or at least moan when she came. Then I decided it was just the way she was wired, and since it didn't interfere with her enjoyment, I wouldn't let it interfere with mine.) There was nothing quiet or ladylike about the way she was thrashing around, though, or the way she clenched around me.

And even less that was ladylike about the way she returned the pleasure once she'd caught her breath. She knows I like a little roughness sometimes, and there was something especially perverse about her pinning me down with her body weight and working me over in a lush Victorian space lavishly and sentimentally decorated for Christmas. Love bites on my breasts and fingernails raking my thighs were just the start, enough to make me wet and squirming and loudly excited.

"Onto all fours, darling," she said huskily. It wasn't an order—we're into sensation, not power-play. I still rolled over obediently and stuck my ass into the air. Why not? I knew what was coming and I knew I'd love it.

With a thwack her hand came down on my butt. I jumped at the sudden sting, even though I was anticipating it, but heat blossomed from the impact immediately, spreading from my butt throughout my whole body. I arched my back up, raising my ass to show I wanted more and was prompted rewarded. The pleasure built as the spanking continued, spiraling from her wicked little hand through my pelvis, right into my cunt. Unlike Lucie, I'm not quiet when I get excited. Pretty soon I was yelping, growling and occasionally giggling from the adrenaline rush.

And pretty soon after that I was begging incoherently.

"What do you want?" she demanded.

"Please…." This was not the time to ask a girl to speak in complete sentences, but if I couldn't say what I wanted, I certainly couldn't string together a concept that complex.

"Please what? Please stop spanking you?"

She said that just as I grunted out another "Please." It was poorly timed—she did stop spanking me.

That provoked one other word: "Bitch."

"Your bitch, though."

I nodded. Then I raised my ass even higher and managed to squeak out, "Please make me come."

She leaned around me, nibbling my ear in passing. "Hey, that was almost articulate. Can't have that."

Her fingers touched my clit, began to circle. With her other hand, she smacked me again, a little faster and sharper now that I was so close.

I howled as I came.

"Happy days," she purred. "Consider this the stocking gift—there's plenty more to follow!"

*

Later, as the storm hit the Cape in earnest, we headed down to Race Point, bundled in our warmest clothes. We clung to each other as we walked, partly against the force of the wind, but mostly because we love to touch, even when the touch is muted through layers of fabric. The crash of the storm-fueled waves and the roar of the wind combined into a white noise that we couldn't talk over. I love the ocean when it's so wild and dramatic, but big areas of beach have been known to wash away when the seas get so rough—we lost entire buildings during the Blizzard of '78—and Lucie finally dragged me away as the snow began to fall thicker and faster.

It was flying fast by the time we got home, obscuring the Christmas lights that brightened the town and the sliver view of the harbor you can usually see from our apartment, the one saving grace of the cramped space. We stripped out of several layers of clothing (pausing frequently to smooch) and made ourselves hot chocolate (pausing frequently to cuddle up against each other and nibble.)

"I'm still chilled," Lucie said after we'd finished our cocoa. "How about a hot shower together?"

That sounded like a good idea, but as I rose to take her up on it, I looked out into the yard and got a better one. Snow fell steady and thick against the twilight—if you could ignore the howling wind, and the fact we couldn't see the house next door despite it being blanketed in a truly scary light display in the shape of an unusually buff Santa waving a Pride flag—it was an idealized Christmas Eve straight out of an old movie. The house and the privacy fence sheltered the back deck from the worst of the wind so it was falling straight down instead of blowing sideways like it was out on the street. "Ever made love in a hot tub in the snow?" I asked.

Lucie grinned. She was already struggling back into her boots before she answered, "Not yet!"

I don't think we'd ever made it downstairs so fast. I made one detour, to turn out the outside speakers so our favorite offbeat versions of holiday classics filled the air, but that took mere seconds since the music mix was already set up.

Certainly we'd never gotten the cover off the tub so efficiently for our guests.

We eased ourselves into the water and melted together, kissing frantically. The snow, a thick veil around the tub, was searingly cold on my skin at first, but within a few minutes the steam from the tub began to do its work and most of the flakes evaporated before they hit us. Some lodged in our hair, cooled our shoulders and necks, but it was just enough to feel good, to remind us of the power of the storm. The wind break wasn't complete, but as long as we stayed mostly underwater, it was all right.

More than all right. It was downright miraculous to be out here on Christmas Eve in the middle of a storm, buoyed up by hot water and surrounded by Loreena McKennitt working her strange magic on "God Rest Ye Merry Gentlemen." All the better to be so in the arms of the woman I love.

My hand slipped between Lucie's thighs, finding a slick warmth, hotter than the water surrounding us. I started to stroke, but then had an inspiration and positioned her over a low jet on her hands and knees. She arched her back in pleasure, dancing multi-colored lights illuminating her expectant face, her short dark hair spangled with snow flakes. "You're evil," she gasped. "Brilliant, but evil."

"Jets are a girl's best friend—I can't believe you never tried it before."

"Never had a chance. We've mostly used the tub when it was full of guests."

She was right, of course. We'd only put in the hot tub early this fall, after a successful summer gave us the spare cash. During the slower parts of the fall and early winter, we'd been busy with post-season repairs and redecorating and getting ready for first Thanksgiving and then Christmas, and collapsing in small, exhausted heaps when we weren't up to our eyebrows in some house project. And we'd gotten used thinking of the tub as the guests' domain, not ours.

Important safety tip: Take time for ourselves more often.

"Like it?"

"Oh, yes."

She was purring, but she still sounded much too coherent. I crouched over her, cupping a breast with one hand, pushing two fingers of the other inside her. So hot and tight, gripping against my hand. Slow in and out fucking, pushing against her swollen G-spot, my thumb on her clit and the relentless caress of the jet. She was so hot that I expected the snow to sizzle as it hit her, but it just melted, joining the water that made her body gleam. "Are you going to come for me?" I whispered in her ear, and she convulsed silently.

I didn't let up, though. Lucie, once she got going, could come for a long time. There's nothing I like better than seeing her becoming utterly boneless with lust, and she certainly obliged, bucking and contracting against my fingers in wave after wave of orgasm and cooing softly.

Until suddenly her noises weren't soft any more. She bucked back against me, almost pushing me over, arched, and howled her pleasure to the snowy night, drowning out the carols, drowning out the howling wind. Drowning out everything but the roar of my blood.

The sound echoed through my clit, ringing me like Santa's sleigh bells, only much sweeter. I'd forgotten, after years with Lucie's quiet ways, how hot a screaming woman can be. (Okay, I hadn't forgotten it. I just hadn't let myself spend too much time being wistful over the one thing missing in a great relationship.) These unfamiliar—yet entirely Lucie—noises galvanized me, pushed me toward the edge as fast as a touch might. I ground myself against Lucie's shuddering body and added my own cries to hers.

We slumped down together, boneless. Somehow, we managed to arrange ourselves so we were supported on the seat and not in danger of drowning. I can't speak for Lucie, but I know in my case, brains weren't involved in the process. I pulled her close, cuddled her still-shuddering form against me.

"Wow," she choked out, and buried her face against my shoulder. A little while later she repeated it. "Wow."

"I've never heard anything that beautiful, love. What broke the dam?"

She shrugged. "I don't know. The jets. You. The contrast between heat and cold. You. This amazing storm. You. Christmas Eve magic. You."

All around us, the roof tops and holiday decorations of Provincetown were disappearing under snow. Our own deck was getting buried except right around the hot tub, and the lights on the backyard trees were obscured by snow. We'd freeze getting back to the apartment, and cleaning up once the storm was over would be backbreaking, and at some point I'd have to think about all the income we weren't getting from the canceled bookings. But for now, safe inside our private Christmas Eve of steam, hot water, and desire, that didn't matter.

"Hearing you let loose like that was the best Christmas gift you could have possibly given me, love," I whispered to Lucie.

She giggled in a floaty way, still on a post-orgasmic high. "That's good," she said. "I didn't have much time to shop. But I think I can give that present over and over—now that I've found it."

Happy Krampusnacht

I unwrapped the newspaper from around another ornament. Slowly, carefully, as if the package contained something delicate and valuable, though that wasn't likely.

A white ceramic ball painted with festive poinsettias. I smiled when I saw it, remembering the craft fair where we'd bought it. Still, a pleasant tension ratcheted up another notch as I hung the pretty ornament on the big Douglas fir, an erotic buzz in my abdomen and pussy.

Where was it? Where was the Krampus ornament?

Ben whooped with glee and I got my answer. He held up the Krampus, a black-clad, bestial figure with a long tongue and a leer, more what most Americans would think of a Halloween decoration than part of a holly-jolly Christmas. "Looks like Stella's been a bad girl this year!"

My pussy clenched, but I managed to reply in a teasing tone. "Like you haven't been a naughty boy."

"Of course I have," he conceded. "Mostly we've misbehaved together and it's been great. But that's not the point. Krampus has decided you're even naughtier than I am. So you're mine tonight." He leered like the ornament, his tongue lolling out. Any other time it would have been comical, but tonight was Saint Nicholas Eve or Krampusnacht, December 5, when Krampus came around to switch naughty children so they'd shape up before Christmas.

And this year, Fate had designated me as the naughty child.

We'd stumbled across our Krampus ornament during a trip to Germany three years ago. We had to buy it. Santa's dark and twisted sidekick who carried a whip and switches appealed both to our perverse senses of humor and our kinky sides.

And perhaps inevitably, given that Ben and I are both switches with the aforementioned perverse sense of humor, the Krampus ornament became part of our holiday tradition. Whoever unpacked the ornament got to "punish" the other, Krampus-style, with switches from the willow tree in the yard.

Last year, I'd found Krampus and discovered that Ben's ass looked wonderful with stripes on it. So wonderful, in fact that when it was his turn to bottom in future, he tasted the cane pretty regularly.

I was so going to pay for that indulgence tonight.

I couldn't wait.

We finished trimming the tree like any other loving couple: sipping eggnog; exclaiming when we unearthed a favorite ornament; singing along in off-key bliss to carols; smooching under the mistletoe. But all the while the pleasant tension vibrated inside me. Krampus was coming. And I'd been a bad, bad girl.

Once the last ornament was in place, I dimmed the lights in the room so we could bask in the tree's sparkle and glow. For a little while, we snuggled on the sofa, vintage Bing Crosby and Frank Sinatra renditions of Christmas classics playing in the background, enjoying the official start of the holiday season. The music and the twinkling lights relaxed me enough that when Ted excused himself and slipped away, I almost forgot to be nervous yet excited.

Without warning, the music changed to Trans-Siberian Orchestra's "Christmas in Sarajevo," festive yet ominous, definitely loud. I jumped, combating a flight-or-flight instinct because I knew in my heart—and the depths of my wet cunt— that I didn't want to do either.

With a wild chortle, Krampus jumped through the doorway. I knew it was Ben in the same black jeans he'd had on earlier, a black turtleneck, a lurid latex devil mask from Halloween, and a hood and capelet we'd created out of shaggy faux fur. I knew it, but that didn't mean I didn't shriek, leap to my feet, and look around wildly for an escape route that the Ben Krampus was blocking.

"Someone's been a very naughty girl," he said, his voice deeper and grittier than usual. As he spoke, he caressed the braided red and black flogger that hung on his belt.

When did we get *that* toy? I didn't remember it. But I suspected that after tonight I'd never forget it.

I froze in my tracks. Then I took a halting step toward Krampus Ben. It wasn't part of the game. I was supposed to struggle and try to escape, like any reasonable woman being chased around by a demon with a fetish for punishment.

But damn it, I have a fetish for punishment as well. My skin tingled with the need to taste that new flogger. And while the devil mask was creepy, especially shadowed by the furry hood, Ben's blue eyes peered out from the red and black face, and the all-black outfit highlighted his slim but fit body.

One step. One more.

Ben's hand shot out. He wore black leather gloves, and when he grabbed my wrist, I could almost believe that his skin felt like that, cool and tough. Almost, not quite. I know leather, intimately, and that was leather, even if I closed my eyes to build the illusion.

He pulled me closer, more roughly than he normally would, even in play. "Got you, you wicked woman." Again with the dark, gravelly voice that freaked me out a little, but also turned me on. He slapped my ass hard with his gloved hand.

While I was still processing the pleasurable pain, he pulled a pillowcase over my head and wrapped something, maybe a scarf, loosely around my neck to hold it in place.

I could still see the flickering Christmas lights, but I was effectively blindfolded, and that the surprise went straight to my pussy.

Which throbbed and lusted even more when Ben grabbed me and got me into a fireman's carry. (I helped as best I could considering I wasn't sure what he was doing.) Once he had me in place, I kicked and screamed obligingly as he carried me upstairs.

He set me on my feet and whipped off the pillowcase. I found myself in a transformed guestroom. Red light bulbs cast a lurid glow. A cauldron we used for Halloween décor fumed and smoked, filled with dry ice. Weird music was playing, bizarre holiday-carol mash-ups we'd found online and downloaded for the hell of it. Right now, I was hearing something about "Sex me, Santa." And in the center of the room was a spanking bench I'd never seen before.

A spanking bench adorned with a gigantic red bow.

I gulped.

"You're too naughty for just coal and a switch. Bad girls like you get a spanking bench all their own."

The bench was gorgeous, the kind of high-end toy we'd often drooled over. I said the only thing I could possibly say: "Thank you, Krampus."

I couldn't see Ben's smile beneath the creepy mask, but his eyes lit up. "Merry Christmas a little early, sweetie," he said in his normal voice. Then he cleared his throat and, once more in the Krampus rumble, he ordered, "Undress, you wicked minx."

I was suppressing a grin as I did—the setting was amazing, the bench was a perfect gift, and Ben's Krampus promised all sorts of nasty fun. My hands trembled from arousal and something fluttered in the pit of my stomach, as if my desire were a living thing fighting for freedom.

I made quick work of my clothes. Ben made equally quick work of positioning me over the spanking bench, ass in the air, and using the attached cuffs to lock me in place. The cuffs were black leather lined with black fur and it didn't take much to pretend that Krampus held me down with magic that was basically an extension of himself.

The spanking bench affected me differently from bending over a bed or chair, as I usually did, or Ben did when it was his turn on the receiving end. Immobilized in a somewhat awkward position, my ass high, my head low, my wet pussy exposed, I felt helpless, deliciously helpless, a prisoner in the anteroom of hell where Krampus entertained his wicked captives.

Lucky me.

Ben began to spank me, his gloved hand smacking hard into my ass. "You're wet," he growled before long. "You know you need correction, don't you? It makes you feel good." I yelped something that vaguely resembled *yes*, followed by a sigh. Even though he started with spanking rather than jumping right to switches and whips, this wasn't a gentle, gradual warm-up. He started out hard and pushed harder with each spank, and soon my ass felt as red as Santa's suit. It throbbed hotly, and my pussy throbbed in time with it. The sensation radiated out from my butt, and soon I felt warm and fuzzy and floaty, despite the occasional yelp of surprise at a particularly hard blow.

"Say it. You need correction and punishment."

No argument there. "Oh God yes, I need this."

"Good. Then it's time for the next stage of your punishment. It takes a devil to beat the devil out of someone, you know."

It was time for the flogger on his belt. He put it under my face, letting me get a good look. The falls were braided, heavy looking but soft. It would be thuddy.

"Kiss it," he snarled. "Prove to me that you accept your punishment. That you crave it."

I pressed my lips to the soft leather, breathing in its luscious, erotic smell. Then I looked up, hoping to see Ben's eyes in Krampus's latex face, but he was already moving behind me.

It was Ben who gently kissed my glowing butt and whispered, "Love you." It was Krampus who used the flogger.

I shuddered under the thuddy blow. My hips tried to press forward, away from the menace (even though I enjoyed the menace), but met vinyl padding and cool wood. He struck again, quickly, while my nerve endings were still reeling and my brain was still out of commission. Then again and again.

After a few more strikes, the pain had become a red haze, but it was a champagne haze, one that lifted me up and carried me along. I lost track of who I was, who Ben was, why he sounded funny when he talked. Everything in my world centered on sensation. Juices slicked my thighs, and my nipples and clit ached with need, and pleasure and pain became the same thing. The room blurred. I sobbed and begged, but I wasn't exactly crying. I was too high on endorphins to know what I craved, whether it was orgasm or some different release. I just moaned, "Please, please, please," over and over again as Ben flogged me, and it was bliss.

By the time he stopped, I was trembling. "Love you," I managed to say.

"You're nearly cured of your wicked ways, naughty girl, but you still have more punishment to endure." Ben's voice reached between my legs and licked. I think he'd forgotten he was supposed to sound like Krampus and he just sounded like Ben in the middle of a heavy scene, but that was still pretty damn sexy.

He reached under a Christmas throw on the bed and pulled out a long, flexible willow branch.

This was going to hurt. In a good way, but even sexy pain is still pain, and canes and switches really burn. I felt my body tighten in anticipation, even though I knew that would just make the switch hurt more. Ben stroked my ass. "Relax," he said, back to the deep, gruff Krampus voice. "It's only pain, girl. Pain lets the bad things loose, so there's more room for Christmas joy and a happy New Year." I was sure that wasn't part of the original Krampus spiel; Krampus was more about keeping kids on the straight and narrow than encouraging bliss. But the words washed over me, soothing my hot, tender spirit if not my ass. My breathing slowed. I willed myself to relax.

And when the switch hit, it was ginger or hot pepper rather than fire, a pleasing burn with a sweet undertone. I couldn't move much, but I did my best to push back, and I whispered, "More, please."

"Oh, there will be more. Twelve, for the twelve days of Christmas. That was one."

Preparing myself, I breathed in. Breathed out. Counted "two" as the next blow fell.

Repeated the process again and again.

Before long, the pain shimmered all over my body and the odd mashed-up carols sounded like the voice of angels. I lost count after seven, but Ben took over for me.

When the last blow fell, harder than the rest, a hot knife followed by sweetness, I didn't know whether to cry or come.

So I did both.

Ben released me, lay me down on the guest bed, under the cheerful holiday throw. Tossed aside the Krampus costume. Stripped off his clothes. Joined me on the bed. He held me as I sobbed, as the room spun around me, as I saw the star of Bethlehem pulse behind my closed eyes.

Still crying, I turned in Ben's arms, reached for his cock, and threw one leg over him. He pushed inside me.

I opened my eyes then, looked into the face of the man I loved, no longer masked. "Happy Krampusnacht," he said to me and I replied with something clever like "Good God, yes." We moved together until we exploded—appropriately enough—during a mash-up that did something sacrilegious and sexy and not entirely musically successful with the "fall on your knees" part of "O Holy Night" melded with Nine Inch Nails' "Closer."

It was only much later, after a nap and wandering back downstairs to fortify ourselves with spiked eggnog, that I put my hands on my hips, glared at Ben, and said, "You cheated!"

"What do you mean?" His attempt to look innocent failed. He might as well have left on the devil mask.

"You didn't have time to set up the guest room after you 'found' the ornament. You must have fixed it somehow so you knew you'd win."

He smirked. "When you had to work late the other night, I went through the box and when I found Krampus, I stowed him in the drawer of the end table."

"Oh you…." I flailed, pretending to smack him a few times. He caught my wrists and drew me in for a kiss.

When we came up for air, I said, "Thank you. It was wonderful, and I love the spanking bench. But I am so going to get you for cheating. Krampus doesn't like people cheating at his sacred rituals. He may need to come back tomorrow night to take care of you. What do you think of that?"

Ben grinned. "I think the spanking bench is adjustable. That's what I think. That and you make an adorable Krampus."

Running Away from Christmas

A plastic Christmas wreath adorned the tour boat's stern, and white lights twinkled around its mast, entirely superfluous in the tropical sunlight, especially with the light glinting on the achingly blue water. The captain was wearing a Santa hat, set on a rakish angle on his shoulder-length dreads. Blue-grey eyes gazed from a handsome, high-cheek-boned, brown face, as if several races and ethnicities had combined in his genes to reach an amazing result. The damn hat looked absurd on him. But not bad, just kitschy. I was pretty sure I'd seen a sexy shirtless Santa on my friend Maurice's tree, hanging between the merman in black leather and the drag queen cat, and he reminded me of that campy ornament. He was wearing a shirt but it hung open, displaying an excellent bare chest.

Not that I thought this guy belonged on Maurice's tree, or in his bed (theoretical bed, since Maurice was married). For a straight woman, I had decent gaydar, thanks to hanging out with Maurice and his self-described fabulous freaky friends. This guy wasn't gay, just getting into the holiday spirit island-style.

"Merry Christmas!" he exclaimed cheerily, his practiced tourism-industry smile not quite reaching his long-lashed eyes. "Glad to see you. I was just about to hang a *Closed for the Holidays* sign on the boat and go help my mum get ready for Christmas Eve dinner."

Duh. I was on the lam from the cold and slush and incessant carols and marketing-induced cheer of New York City but the locals were still celebrating Christmas. December was blissfully warm and sunny here in Provo, though—Providenciales, in the Turks and Caicos Islands chain—and you couldn't hang a wreath on a beach or pipe canned carols underwater to intrude on my snorkeling adventures, so I'd almost forgotten the date. "Sorry," I mumbled. "Time got away with me. Listen, if you want to be with family, I'll come back…not tomorrow obviously, but whenever you'll be running tours again."

"December 27. My cousins on North Cay have a party on Boxing Day and I'll be using the boat to ferry everyone over. But we can tour today, since you're here." He smiled again, and this time it reached his eyes. "If I show up too early, my mum will rope me into cleaning and decorating cookies and tidying the yard. Much rather give a pretty lady a private tour. I can show you my favorite secret beach, which I don't do for just anyone."

"You're good," I admitted, his infectious smile and charming accent, British via the Caribbean, getting through my New Yorker's natural skepticism. "I'll even pretend it's true about the secret beach."

"It is. Unspoken pact among the locals. Gotta keep something sacred. I'm Tom, by the way."

"Anna."

He extended his hand to help me aboard. I took it, not because I needed the help, but because I wanted to touch him. He was attractive, with a chest that Captain America would envy and a natural elegance (even in shorts, an unbuttoned shirt, and the Santa hat) that Maurice and his friends would spend big bucks to emulate. And if he smiled and flirted because it was part of his job, he did it well and I might as well have fun with it. Maurice and his husband would be disappointed if I didn't come back with a good flirtation story, if not tales of wild vacation flings.

That is, if they'd forgiven me by the time I got home.

Tom held my hand just a little longer than he needed to once I was safely on the deck of the catamaran. Maybe his charm and the hint of flirtation wasn't just marketing. And the part that was marketing worked well. The notion of having that smile and those lovely muscles to myself for a few hours, on top of the pleasure of a sailing tour around the island, made me happy to hand over my payment.

I didn't know a thing about sailing beyond "sailboats are pretty" so I kept out of the way as Tom cast off. I asked questions that I hoped didn't make me sound like a complete moron, and he answered patiently. As we got underway, though, I stopped talking and tore my eyes away from his cute butt and broad shoulders so I could look at the other scenery. For my first two days on the island, I'd been content to hang out on the resort's beach and snorkel at the reef that protected it. I'd even eaten at the resort instead of venturing farther afield. Usually I'm all about the local color when I'm traveling, but I'd been stuck in the winter doldrums even though I'd left winter behind in Manhattan. Now I was finally relaxed enough to want to see the place I'd come so far to visit, not just the stretch of beach closest to the resort.

"Beautiful," I breathed as we reached open water and I could look back at the island behind us.

"Wait until you see the other side of the island."

And he was right. The far side of the island was less developed, with few all-inclusive resorts running down to its sandy beaches, and it was prettier yet. The water was the startling blue you see in tourism brochures and figure had to be product of Photoshop, and it was so clear that I could see brightly colored fish and the occasional ray right from the boat. Provo was flat and green, a textbook tropical island, bordered with pristine beaches that dazzled my eyes as they gleamed in the sun. "The tourist websites weren't lying, for once. The whole island is surrounded by beaches as white as snow." I chuckled and added, "Movie snow, that is. Real-life snow isn't that clean and white."

Tom pulled a sad face that would have done credit to a small boy who'd just learned Santa wasn't real. "That's right. Crush my illusions. I've never seen snow. Now I may never bother."

"There, there." I patted him on the broad shoulder as if he was that small boy. He didn't feel like a small boy, though, and that was, of course, why I did it. Then I pulled my hand back because it felt too good on his skin. "Don't listen to me. I'm a cynical New Yorker. City snow gets gray and nasty almost before it hits the ground. I'm sure you can find places where it's as pretty as in the movies. But why would you want to? You live in paradise and you get paid to bring people to the best parts of it. Why go somewhere cold and snowy?"

"I'd like to have a white Christmas for once, just to see what it's like. Have a proper Christmas tree, not a plastic one, not a palm tree or banana tree with lights strung on it, but a big old pine that smells good. Carol from house to house while the snow falls."

"A white sandy beach is my favorite kind of white Christmas. The snowy kind is highly overrated. Why do you think I'm here for the holidays?"

For a long moment, I stared at the brilliant water and hoped he didn't answer. I'd said way too much, and not the important parts. And I was still standing too close, even though I'd moved my hand off his skin. I forced myself to take a few more steps away and grab a Turk's Head beer from the cooler. I didn't care for beer all that much, but I needed something to do with my hands because otherwise, I might just start touching Tom again and that was, at best, rude.

Maybe this tour hadn't been such a great idea, despite the gorgeous day, the postcard-worthy beauty, and the hot captain. It was way too easy to get intense and awkward when there were just two of you on the boat.

"I'd wondered about that," Tom said, as if after a long thought. "Most of the tourists who stay here over Christmas are with their families or their lovers, but you're alone. So I figure maybe you're Jewish or something and escaping all the fuss. I love Christmas, but it must be a bore if it's not your holiday."

"Pretty much it. Not Jewish, though," I added, not that it was any of his business. "Just not into the whole thing, and the way everyone starts planning for it in, like, October. And tired of everyone assuming I wanted to do the whole family thing on Christmas when I don't. You know: Stress over gifts. Listen to nieces and nephews whine because they didn't get exactly what they wanted, or because it's snowing, or because it's not snowing, or basically because they're overexcited, overtired little kids who can't help being cranky. Have your mom interrogate you about when you're getting married. Listen to your uncle spew the same homophobic, bigoted rant he gives every time he has a few drinks and never mind that your best friend is a gay black guy. My own family finally stopped asking me to come home, but now all my friends assume I want to be with their damn families. So I'm here instead."

Tom was staring at me like I'd grown a second head, and after that outburst I didn't blame him. Hell, I wasn't sure I *hadn't* grown a second head, one that spilled all my angst to a stranger. Where was my New York ironic detachment?

To my horror, I realized I was crying. I didn't even know why. "Sorry," I muttered, searching desperately for a tissue I didn't have in the pocket of my shorts.

Suddenly Tom's arms were around me and he was making soothing noises in my ear. His arms felt good around me, strong and sure, and even though I knew I ought to hold myself a little stiff and aloof, I found myself snuggling against his chest, feeling safer and more secure than I had any right to with a stranger. Damn man was made for snuggling against. And no doubt for other activities that required close physical proximity, a thought that started to cut through the weird holiday funk that made me all weepy. Not enough that I stopped crying, but enough that tears or no tears, my nipples perked up against my tankini top, and a party started organizing in the bikini bottoms I wore under my shorts. Maybe we could stay like this until I calmed down and then we could sink down onto the deck and…

Run aground on one of the many reefs in the area? Maybe not such a plan.

I glanced nervously at the abandoned steering wheel—it probably had another name on a boat but I didn't know it. "Don't worry. We're safe for while," he whispered. "Just relax. Let it out."

"Don't want to. It's stupid. I'm on a sailboat in one of the most beautiful places I've ever been, drinking a beer and chatting with the handsome captain. It makes no sense that I'm crying."

"It'll make sense eventually. Just hope it wasn't something I said."

I shook my head, probably smearing tears and snot on his chest. "Not you. Me." It was starting to come together and it was embarrassing to admit, but I'd already embarrassed myself in front of Tom. It might help to clear my head if I talked about it, and Tom, for whatever reason, was willing to listen. "I have a great career, terrific friends, a life that lets me do things like take off to Provo for ten days because I feel like it. I'm single, but for now that's okay. Someday I hope I meet someone for the long haul, but I'm not in a hurry. I don't want kids, so I don't have that whole biological pressure going on and I can be patient until the right person comes along. But Christmas is all family, family, snow, and more family, and songs about family and snow and I feel like I *should* want something different at Christmas. It makes me depressed, and it makes me angry that I'm depressed. I used to have Maurice, who didn't even speak to his parents, and I certainly wouldn't bring him home to hang with my uncle the ranting racist homophobe, so we'd do Christmas together. Order Thai, make cookies, drink eggnog, watch a marathon of movies with shirtless men in them."

Tom nodded, "I guess it depends on your family. Mine all spends a lot of time together anyway, but I know a lot of folks say the big family get-togethers are more stress than they're worth."

"And then Maurice went and got *married*. To a guy who has a big, close family near Buffalo, where it's been snowing since September. Okay, slight exaggeration, but I'm pretty sure it snowed on Halloween. And they wanted me to come with them and have a white Christmas."

"And you almost did it, didn't you?"

Damn, Tom was perceptive. Too perceptive. "Thought about it. I love Maurice and I like Patrick and I thought it might be fun for a change. But Patrick has literally thirteen nieces and nephews, and they're definitely in the snow belt. So I chickened out, and Maurice and I had a fight because he thought I was dissing Patrick, which I wasn't. I'm just nervous about being snowbound with a bunch of people I don't know, many of whom are under ten. And I didn't want to go to my family and deal with their nonsense, but they'd expect me to if I wasn't with Maurice. So I decided to come here instead and now my parents are annoyed, too. I've been second-guessing myself ever since. Maybe a white Christmas with Patrick's family or a holiday with the folks wouldn't have been so bad. At least I wouldn't have hurt anyone's feelings."

"Maybe," Tom conceded, "and maybe next year you'll do one or the other. But for now, you're on Provo, so enjoy your time here. Hang on a minute." He stepped back to the helm. "We're almost there."

"Where?"

"Nan's Cay. The private beach I was talking about."

I looked up and what remained of my self-inflicted misery dissolved like snow hitting a subway grate when I saw the beautiful little cay before us. It was tiny, maybe city-block-sized, but jewellike in its miniature perfection. An absolutely opulent white beach, a few strategically placed palm trees, and not much else. And it was utterly deserted. "Wow," I breathed. "You certainly deliver."

Once we made our way onto the beach, I grabbed a handful of warm, soft sand and let it run between my fingers while

Tom spread out a blanket and opened a couple of bottles of beer for us. "Now this is what I call a white Christmas." I ran back into the shallows, where I whirled joyously, letting water splash around me. Then I ran back to Tom. "Why isn't everyone in the world here?"

"It's tiny and out of the way, and the snorkeling isn't spectacular here. Good, but not spectacular. With so many lovely beaches right on Provo, not many people make the trip. But it's a great place to go when you're feeling stressed."

"Was it that obvious I was a stress case even before I spilled my guts? Because you'd been talking about this place all along."

Tom laughed. "Thought you might be, but mostly it was for me. I love Christmas, but the holidays can be stressful even in paradise. Mum's going crazy getting the house ready, Dad's going crazy cooking, and they'll be up all night wrapping presents for my sisters' kids. And by this time tomorrow, one of the kids will be sick on sweets, another will be crying, the rest will be running around like nutters, one of my sisters will be bickering with her husband, and Aunt Dahlia will be drunk."

"Maybe we should just stay here. Might be safer."

"Wouldn't miss the family shindig for the world, but it's good to get some quiet time beforehand. Helps me stay cool when things get crazy." Tom moved a step closer. Damn, he was a sexy man. "And I don't think it would be safer to stay here. Might not be safe at all. You are one pretty lady, and you look like you need some fun. And I was trying to be all gentlemanly at the time, since you'd been crying, but I swore I heard you call me handsome."

I could have pretended I hadn't said it, or that I'd been joking around to lighten my mood.

But what the hell. I was alone on a desert island with a gorgeous man and he was absolutely right: I needed some fun. I'd let myself get way too wound up over this Christmas fiasco, the tension with Maurice, the knowledge I was disappointing my family, even if it was to protect my own sanity.

And Tom looked like he would definitely be fun.

"I was just calling it like I see it. You're handsome. You're sexy. And it's a sad testament to how stressed I was that I was actually crying when you were holding me instead of doing this." I crossed the slight distance between us, wrapped my arms around him, and kissed him for all I was worth.

He didn't hesitate, not even a second of "what the hell?" before he yielded to "hell yeah." I'd felt secure when he held me before, but now I felt wonderfully reckless and recklessly wonderful. I put a lot into that kiss, desire, need, and a weird sense of connection. Not that I imagined Tom was the love of my life (it would be damn inconvenient if he turned out to be) but I liked the guy as well as lusting after him. More than that, I trusted him. Not enough to give him my passwords or Social Security number, but enough to spill my guts to him, which is more than I'd do for some people I'd trust with my finances.

As we kissed, I plucked off the Santa hat and flung it into the sand. It had made me smile, sure, but I wasn't about to have sex with a guy in a Santa hat.

And we were going to have sex.

Neither of us was wearing much to start with. As the kiss deepened, it was easy for me to slide my hands into the waistband of his shorts and caress his muscular bare ass. He wasn't wearing underwear, and I dearly wanted to slide my hand over to his cock, or just unzip him, but I didn't want to rush things too much. Besides, I got a bit distracted when he untied my tankini top and tossed it into the soft sand, leaving me naked to the waist, my breasts at the mercy of his clever, work-hardened hands.

After that, it was easy for him to kiss and caress his way down my body. He sucked and licked and bit at my nipples, of course, did that until I was as wet as if we'd gone swimming in that clear blue water, but he also nuzzled my armpits, and traced my collarbone and ribs with his tongue, until the skin came alive and I was seeing stars blizzarding behind my eyelids. He even tongued my navel, a sensual, surprising caress. No one had ever done that before, and I was hardly a blushing innocent. At home, I might have been self-conscious if a guy paid that much attention to my belly, start worrying about a bit of extra padding instead of enjoying the moment. But in the same way I could spill my guts to Tom, I could enjoy him enjoying a part of me I consider imperfect. And it felt wonderful. Okay, it tickled a little, but it still felt wonderful.

By the time he unzipped my shorts and slithered them and my bikini bottoms off, I was half out of my mind, ready to peel his shorts off and see how quickly I could get his cock inside. But he was having none of that. Instead he knelt in sand white as snow, wrapped his arms around my hips, and buried his face between my legs. I drew in a quick breath at the first hot flick of his tongue on my swollen clit. Then I widened my stance in the sand to allow him easier access.

His big hands grasped my ass. He could have made it feel controlling, either in a fun, sexily dominant way or in a weird, creepy way, but he didn't. It felt secure, protective. I was naked under the Caribbean sun on Christmas Eve with a man I hadn't known a few hours ago, which was pretty edgy, and yet

I felt safe. Nervous in that new-adventure way, but no more so than I had been about spending Christmas on my own on Providenciales. Maybe the holidays, or rather my own dumb problems with the holidays, had made me a little insane.

Once his tongue and lips and my clit began to get better acquainted, I stopped trying to analyze my own behavior. Maybe I was crazy, but I'd take this kind of insanity over the insanity I'd be suffering at home at the moment—most likely battling cranky crowds to pick up a last-minute gift or a bottle of wine. At least this craziness felt really, really good. Pleasure zapped my clit and pussy each time he licked me, surged when he suckled my clit. Pleasure was radiating outward, hot and moist, thawing all the secret places a grim New York fall and winter had frozen to gray city ice. Beautiful blue waves lapped at the shore, and Tom lapped at me. My abs quivered and turned liquid. My knees turned to jelly, then to water. I would have flowed away without Tom's supportive arms, and I understood now why I'd felt so safe in his embrace. He might be pushing me to the edge, but he wouldn't let me fall.

Not for real, not onto my ass in the sand.

Instead, he took me to the edge of orgasm and hold me there, quivering, until I was sobbing and begging much more loudly than I'd normally let myself when the people next door were only fifteen feet away, separated by a not-thick-enough wall. Only then did he give me that last skilful lick I needed to leap off the cliff.

I fell, but he held me up. I screwed my eyes shut and saw dancing lights like the ultimate Christmas tree. And when my knees got too weak and the storm of sensation howling inside me became too strong, Tom eased me onto the blanket.

He lay over me in push-up position, holding up his weight with his strong arms. Sweat gleamed on his skin, polishing him so he looked like a sculpture, and I could see my juices around his full mouth.

He still wore his shorts. I reached for the zipper. "You sure?" he asked, looking almost shy.

"God, yes. I wanted you naked about thirty seconds after meeting you." Sanity returned for a second, overriding the urgent hurry of my cunt. "You got a condom?"

I could see sanity returning for him, too. "God, I hope so. They'd be on the boat." He sprang to his feet and ran back to the boat, splashing through the shallow water. I wished for binoculars so I could get a better view of his muscles shifting under his skin as he climbed aboard.

By the time he came back, the precious packet in hand, wearing nothing but a smile of anticipation, I was humming to myself. He laughed as he sank down onto his knees between my open legs. "Deck the Halls? Thought you hated Christmas."

"You're the best gift ever, wrapped for me and everything. It's given me back my Christmas spirit." I glanced at the bright red condom wrapper on the blanket. "You even picked a seasonal color." I picked up the Santa hat, shook sand out of it, and placed it on his head. "So let's get holly and jolly and have a white-sand Christmas." Silly, sure, but I think I could be forgiven, considering my brains had been dribbling out my ears a little while before.

And as soon as Tom entered me, they were again.

He felt so good in me, his cock big and hard and hitting all the right places, his body so strong and dark and perfect. I couldn't break down how much of the experience was Tom's physical beauty and how much was the glorious setting and the freedom of being so far from my ordinary life, or the sheer weird poetry of fucking a stranger on a Caribbean beach on Christmas Eve. I know all these factors played a part in opening me to the pleasure. But Tom was simply good at fucking, knew how to touch a woman, how to kiss, how to work magic with his hands and tongue and cock. Beyond that, he made me feel, while we were together, like I was the only woman on earth.

I'm not naïve. A guy didn't get this skilled, either at the sex or at the games leading up to getting naked with someone, without plenty of practice. If he hadn't taken other women to this perfect beach, it was because he'd been with them in his house, or their place, or in the cramped cabin of the catamaran, or some other beach. But I hadn't exactly spent time waiting for Mr. Perfect when there were plenty of delightful Mr. Perfectly Funs around. That was why I knew it was a real gift to use all that experience and still see each partner and each act of sex as a unique, precious thing.

I'm not so good at that myself, but Tom was, good enough that for the time I was under him, his cock inside me, nothing else mattered.

Because I could tell nothing else mattered for him, just me and Tom and the pleasure we were giving each other.

It wasn't perfect. First times with a new lover never are. There were awkward moments where he went a little too hard for my comfort before he caught my rhythm and settled into deliciously slow, purposeful strokes, a few awkward moments when I was unaccountably nervous about touching him, as if his body might shatter if I stroked his impossibly beautiful skin. In the back of my mind, I realized that lovely white sand was going to chafe in unfortunate places, although I wasn't feeling that now, was feeling only Tom's cock moving in me, Tom's weight over, Tom's sweat-slicked skin under my hands and his lips on mine.

But imperfections only added to the perfection, and for some reason I thought of the vintage ornaments on my mom's tree—not valuable antiques, just battered Santas and faded glass balls and one-winged angels from her childhood and even my grandparents', imperfect and precious.

We kissed nearly the whole time he was in me, deep, desperate kisses like we were teenagers again, or a romantic, committed couple who'd been apart way too long. We kissed, and he moved inside me and I wrapped my legs around his slim hips and pushed up against him and sang a carol of hallelujahs to myself as I came and came.

He held out for a long time, but in the end he shattered, crying out wordlessly to a blue sky now tinted with the first hints of sunset. He pressed his lips to my forehead, held me close and for a few brief seconds, I think he honestly loved me and I honestly loved him. Nothing substantial, nothing that would last, but it felt real.

We cuddled briefly, cleaned up with a swim in the rose-streaked azure water, snacked on slightly soggy sandwiches from the cooler.

We didn't talk much, either then or on the sail back. Curiously, it didn't feel awkward, more like a comfortable quiet time with Maurice, just hanging out and not needing to talk at that particular moment, secure in the knowledge that we could start chatting again whenever we needed to.

It wasn't permanent, any more than the flood of affection on the beach had been. But we had it now, and that was good enough.

Awkwardness reared its ugly head when we got back to port. "I feel like we should go to dinner or something," Tom said, holding my hand. "But…"

"It's Christmas Eve and your family's expecting you. I understand." I smiled as I said it, but I felt oddly bereft.

"You should come over tonight."

"We're not exactly at the meeting-the-parents stage. I don't even know your last name. And I'm sure your parents wouldn't be thrilled with a last-minute guest on Christmas Eve."

He laughed. "Well, yeah, Mum would kill me. But it also seemed rude not to ask."

I hugged him. He was seriously adorable, almost too good for a vacation fling. "Thank you for thinking of it. And Merry Christmas."

"Same to you." He kissed me, a gentle, tender kiss that felt like it belonged in a real relationship. "Say, about tomorrow…"

"No way. Not spending Christmas with your family. I'm sure they're lovely, but I can't imagine anything more awkward." I wasn't looking forward to a quiet Christmas alone as much as I had been, but going to my hookup's family? No thanks.

Tom pulled me closer. "Not that. I was just thinking…I love my family, but the house is awfully small when the whole crew's there. Usually I escape after dinner for a bit, go sailing. Want to come with me? I'll bring a bottle of something nice and some home-cooked leftovers. We can celebrate a white Christmas on Nan's Cay."

By the way his cock was jutting into me, I knew exactly what kind of celebration he had in mind—and I heartily approved. "Absolutely. Bring the Santa hat.

Sophie Mouette

A Bird in the Hand

"**I** don't be*lieve* it!"

My roommate Donna stared at me, spoon halfway to her mouth and dripping milk and Cheerios. "What's wrong?"

I slammed the New England Birdwatcher's Association newsletter onto the kitchen table. "That—that Al Johnson guy! He beat me to the Barrow's Goldeneye! Dammit! He's going to win the award, the tweeter-head."

"I'm sorry, CeCe," Donna said. "But where the hell did he see a Barrow's Goldeneye at this time of year?"

"Provincetown," I snarled.

I'd won NEBA's annual Top Birder contest for three years running, and I wasn't happy about losing the title to some upstart newbie from P-Town.

I don't know where this Al Johnson had come from, but he'd started showing up in the NEBA newsletter in March this year, and we'd been neck-and-neck when it came to bird sightings throughout the year.

All I needed was a Barrow's Goldeneye and a common moorhen—which weren't common at all—to win, and I thought I'd nail those at the Winter Bird Watch.

Now he was ahead of me.

This meant war.

*

At the reception the night before the Winter Bird Watch, I wore a slinky little crimson strapless number, just in case. I had my doubts about its effectiveness; given where Al lived, he was unlikely to fly in my formation, if you know what I mean.

I had a mental picture of what Al must look like: slender, a little nebbish. Frown lines between his brows. A little fluttery with his hands, like my fabulous gay friend Logan.

I scanned the crowd in the Provincetown Inn's reception room, shivering a little when I got too close to the door, but there was nobody there I didn't know. I relaxed, just a little. Maybe he'd gone home for the holidays.

What I should have been thinking was, and maybe a roseate spoonbill will land in front of my camera tomorrow and make me the toast of NEBA.

You know what they say about "assume"....

*

The next day, Donna and I were up before sunrise. I bundled up in thermal silk underwear, boots, scarf, gloves, hat, the works.

Camera, check. Water, check. Cell phone, check. Binoculars, check.

Acme Portable Hole to drop in front of Al Johnson so I could beat him to the interesting birds—not a check, but if it actually existed, it would have been in my pack.

Donna went through the same drill, although with a few more camera-related bits and probably without the yearning for the Portable Hole. Because she's more a nature photographer than a birder, we can be roommates without bloodshed, because she never, ever spots a bird before I do.

We headed out toward the Province Lands parking lot at the Cape Cod National Seashore, where NEBA members gathered before scattering to see what avian excitement the forest, the dunes, and the shore might offer. We did this every winter at a different spot in New England. Last year we'd hit northern Vermont, where I'd scored a golden eagle.

I wasn't expecting anything that big and dramatic here, but I had high hopes for a moorhen and a pine grosbeak, and maybe, if I got very, very lucky, a marbled godwit. I'd settle for a Hudsonian godwit, even. They weren't as rare, but it had been years since I'd seen one.

As long as Al Johnson didn't beat me to it.

I sized up the gathered crowd. "We should have brought Logan," I whispered to Donna. My breath clouded in the air. It wasn't bad for December in Massachusetts—just above freezing and only a little windy—but I was looking forward to getting moving.

"Logan? Up at this hour, and out in the cold? I don't think so. If he's awake this early, it's because he hasn't gone to sleep yet."

"But he's so pretty. He'd be a good distraction." I gestured toward a small cluster of what appeared to be unattached gay men, any one of whom might be Al.

Donna shook her head. "It doesn't have to be a competition, CeCe."

"Of course it does. It's the NEBA Annual Birdspotting Award. 'Award' implies 'competition.'" Sheez. Okay, I'd had birding rivals before, but it was mostly friendly, with lots of mostly joking rivalry and e-mailing to gloat when one of us spotted something new and exciting.

Al was just The Enemy—and he was getting on my last nerve.

"Hey." Donna elbowed me. "Hot guy at ten o'clock. As in hot enough I'm even noticing."

Donna *definitely* didn't fly in the same formation that I did, which was another reason we got along as roommates— we left each other's dates alone.

Oh. My. God. Put him on my life list and call me a happy birder. Look at that glossy plumage…

Dark hair so thick my hands itched to run through it, feather its thick softness between my fingers. Under the bulk of LL Bean's finest, I could make out broad shoulders and a solid build—not beefy, but lean and taut. Okay, maybe I was extrapolating a little bit.

But those cheekbones bespoke tautness elsewhere, and then there were those startling blue eyes….

Various parts of my body fluttered.

And he was coming this way, with a definite flirtatious smile on his face.

I had never, ever, in my life been so glad my bestest girl-friend was a dyke.

"Hi," he said, extending his hand. "I'm Mac—and my friends just called to say they're down with flu and I'm on my own. Mind if I team up with you?"

"CeCe, and not at all."

Could be true, could be a transparent excuse to introduce himself. I didn't much care. A hunk—a hunk with the kind of binoculars you don't have if you're a clueless beginner—would make the Winter Bird Watch all that more fun.

As long as I didn't spend more time looking at his tailfeathers than the birds', but I trusted my self-control. Flirt before, flirt after, watch birds during.

We locked eyes. I smiled. So did he. Donna, mostly ignored by both of us, took the hint and excused herself to join some other friends.

A small flock of mergansers flew overhead.

Mac and I both looked up, binoculars at the ready. I could feel the thrill of the hunt warming me. Really. The thrill of the hunt. That's what was causing the heat deep in my belly.

"Common?" he asked, getting ready to check them off.

"Yeah…no…wait, they're hooded!" Which weren't exactly rare birds, but it was rare to see them at this time of year on the Cape.

"Excellent." A deep dimple appeared on his left cheek. I felt that fluttering again.

Yeah, it would be okay. The attraction was there, all right, but we had our priorities in line.

The birds came first.

Yeah, right.

*

The dawn's pink had faded from the sky, leaving behind a cold, lowering gray, but I was feeling pretty damn good despite a cold nose and ears.

Buried under thermal layers, my nipples peaked for reasons not related to the season.

Certain other parts of me were warmer. Tingly, even.

Mac and I had spotted thirty species so far, including a few rarities, and our total count was about three hundred individual birds. We hadn't chatted a lot—didn't want to scare off our targets—but there'd been a lot of significant eye contact and sly smiles, when we weren't staring into trees or off into the choppy water, a lot of standing closer to each other than really necessary and brushing of hands when I showed him where that grosbeak was or he pointed out the unusual sparrow. Our infrequent hushed tones made things seem all the more intimate.

Plus there was always that sitting-real-close-to-maximize-body-heat thing.

Non-birders think what we do is boring. They just don't get it. It's the thrill of the chase, the challenge of the hunt. Now, for us, it had gone beyond just being about the birds. Mac and I had embarked on our own thrilling chase.

In fact, while we'd done really well on our sightings, I had a feeling we'd missed a few birds because we were too busy flirting.

And as long as Al Johnson, whoever he was, missed them too, I was fine with that. Birds may come and go, but I hadn't had a human-male sighting this good in a long time.

So when we took a break—he pulled out a Thermos of coffee, I offered trail mix and energy bars—I asked, "I can't believe we've never met. Which region are you in?"

"This one. I'm pretty new here, though—just moved up from Pennsylvania in February when I got a job at the Truro hospital. Always wanted to live by the ocean."

Oh. Crap. My mental database started running triple-time.

Hadn't the first newsletter that mentioned damnable Al Johnson also mentioned his long affiliation with Pennsylvania Audubon?

And hadn't his first sighting appeared in the March newsletter?

But the name was wrong. Couldn't be. Must be a coincidence.

Assume nothing.

"You know," I said, fishing desperately, "we never did the full introduction thing. My grandma must be doing backflips. I'm CeCe Harrington, from Swampscott. And before you ask, because people always do, CeCe's short for Cecilia Clarice, but if you ever call me that, I'll punch you."

That cheeky dimple again. "If we're going for the whole double-barreled thing, I'm Albert MacKenzie Johnson Junior."

"Albert?"

"Our real names could be on a Victorian gravestone together. My father's Al, so I became Mac."

"You're Al Johnson." My mental nebbish superimposed itself over Mac's handsome face and hot bod, then melted away like an icicle caught in an early thaw. It was impossible to remember the old picture with the true one undressing me with his eyes.

Oblivious to the icy tone of my voice, he shrugged and said, "I could kill the newsletter editor. I told him about fifty times that I prefer Mac."

"Al Johnson the Goldeneye stealer."

"That sounds very James Bond." He grinned, an adorable lopsided grin that normally would have made me melt like that icicle, but this time just made me madder.

Why did he have be good looking and charming? The guy I'd imagined would have been easier to dismiss…

…and wouldn't have been flirting with me.

"You know, I've been wanting to meet you," he said. "Everyone told me about you and your incredible eye…which you have. Incredible eyes, I might add."

I wanted to soften toward him. My body was thawing. I mean, really, flattery won't get you everywhere, but it will get you a long way.

But I was still pissed about that Barrow's Goldeneye. And the nesting vultures this summer. And a half dozen other local rarities that he got to see first.

For the first time in hours I was aware of the chill, of the way the sky had darkened with clouds. I saw the play of emotions in his eyes, and realized I hadn't responded to his compliment, and he probably thought he'd been shot down like an unlucky waterfowl during duck season.

Then, in the distance, we heard a cry.

"Moorhen!" we said simultaneously.

We both started to move in its direction. "No, you don't," I said, elbowing him. "I'm getting to this one first."

"Why don't we try to spot it together? Turn in the sighting jointly?"

I paused for a second. Was he for real?

"We both heard it. Why fight over it?"

It was the principle of the thing, that's why. And I swear that's why I played dirty.

I grabbed his fleece collar, yanked him towards me, and kissed him.

I stroked my tongue along his, tasting the coffee we'd shared and the mint of his lip balm. His lips were surprisingly warm, surprisingly supple. He got over his shock quickly, matching my movements.

Sparkles of arousal flared through my body, at all the good spots. Without meaning to, I rose onto tiptoes, buoyed by the desire growing between my legs.

Wait. I wasn't supposed to be getting all horny over a kiss hot enough to set the bare, damp trees on fire. I was supposed to be…mmm…

My body insisted I was supposed to be doing just this, and hopefully more, very soon.

The call of the moorhen finally broke the spell.

I lightened the kisses, teasing, nipping, and Mac followed suit, and then I pulled back and said "See ya" and bolted in the direction of the bird's cry.

"What the—hey!" His indignant shout bounced off my departing back.

I figured I'd have enough of a head start to at least spot the bird a few seconds before him, and even those few seconds would be enough. Slogging through the snow wasn't easy with my sex swollen and needy, but I did my best. Just when I thought I'd caught a glimpse of the moorhen's distinctive red face when I heard another cry—of pain.

I'm competitive, not heartless. I didn't have to think twice about spinning around and heading back.

Mac had caught his foot in a tangled root hidden beneath the blanket of snow and twisted his ankle. By the time I dropped to my knees at his side, he was probing beneath the edges of his hiking boot.

"Just a sprain," he pronounced. "Help me over to that log there. I'll wait while you finish up your day."

"Don't be ridiculous," I said. "You need to get home."

"But you haven't seen—"

"If you haven't noticed, the temperature's dropped; there's a storm brewing. If you sit here, you'll freeze. C'mon."

He used a branch for leverage, and between that and his arm draped over me, we managed to make slow but steady progress back to the parking area. Most of the cars were gone when we got there; Donna had called me earlier to say she and the other girls were probably leaving early because of the weather, and Mac had said he could drive me to the hotel for the banquet and awards ceremony.

We'd danced around the unspoken idea that my room would be just upstairs in the hotel, but that was before I knew that Al was Mac, or Mac was Al, or whatever.

To be honest, I was forgetting why I'd been so worked up. I'd built Al up in my mind as an interloper, an enemy, but Mac wasn't like that mental picture at all.

It irked the hell out of me, but deep down, I was beginning to see the positive aspects of changing my opinion.

Thankfully Mac's house was only one story, and other than hopping two steps up onto the porch, it was easy to get him inside and onto the living room sofa with an ottoman propping up his injured foot.

I dumped my outer gear in his foyer and found an ice pack in the freezer for him. I eased off his boot and woolen sock. His ankle was swollen and purpling, and he hissed when I set the ice pack on it.

"CeCe, thank you," he said. "You've been wonderful. Now get out of here—you're going to miss winning your award."

Funny, but the award didn't seem to mean as much right now. Fact was, I wanted to spend more time with Mac.

"Eh," I said. "They're probably all sick of watching me accept the prize. And oh God, but the slide shows are deathly boring. You, on the other hand, have a widescreen TV and an impressive-looking DVD collection. I'm going to make coffee; why don't you order in some Chinese? Hot-and-sour soup sounds really great right now."

We never did get around to a movie. One minute I was licking plum sauce off my fingers, and the next he was licking plum sauce off my fingers, his eyes locked with mine and making all sorts of promises about what his delightful tongue could do on other parts of my body.

The food abandoned, I threw a leg over his and settled down for some serious canoodling.

I indulged in the fantasy I'd harbored when I'd first seen him, threading my fingers through his soft, thick hair. All the better to pull him closer.

When he tugged my silk underwear top out of my waistband, I couldn't suppress a moan. His hands, large and warm, roamed across the bare skin of my back, his thumbs sliding across my ribcage and toying with the sensitive undercurve of my breasts.

I wanted more. Needed more. I peeled off the shirt.

When he covered my breasts with his hands, I shivered, not from cold but from aching desire. My nipples strained against his palms. I leaned forward, bracing my hands on the back of the sofa. Just a suggestion…

He didn't need to be asked twice. He sucked one rosy bud into his mouth, used his talented fingers to toy with the other. I squirmed in his lap, unable to keep still. Through two pairs of jeans I felt the hard length of him press along me, and the more I wriggled, the more his hips moved, until I was on the cusp of coming just from those sensations alone.

Tempting. But I'm stubborn, and I wanted the greater prize.

He said condoms were in the medicine cabinet, and I made it there and back to the living room in record time. Peeling off his jeans without hurting his ankle was delicate work, but we were both eager for the same result.

Finally he was naked, and I couldn't resist dipping my head to taste the drop of fluid that leaked from the tip of his reddened cock, like a hummingbird drawn to sweet nectar, before rolling the condom down him with long, firm strokes.

Then I straddled him again, and let the head of his cock rub against my slick folds and stroke against my clit, teasing myself, teasing him, until I was gasping and he was groaning and neither of us wanted to wait any longer.

I sank down. The feel of him sliding into me was like the coming of spring: relief, joy, ecstasy. He took my breasts in his hands again, urging me on. With a grace I hadn't realized I had, I found the perfect motion of posting and rocking that did wonderful things to my G-spot and apparently doing happy things for Mac, too.

My thighs trembled, but there was no way I could stop now. When Mac slipped a hand between us to stroke my clit, I went off like a Christmas cracker, convulsing against his thick length and bringing him right over the edge with me.

I rested my head on his shoulder, gulping for air. My heart rate had almost returned to normal when it shot back up again, thanks to what I saw out the window behind him.

"I don't effing believe it."

"What?" He twisted around to see.

A formerly elusive common moorhen strolled through his snow-dusted backyard as if it owned the place, its red face gleaming in the glow of a nearby streetlight.

"You spotted it first," Mac said. "You win."

I responded with a twitch of my hips that made his eyes widen.

"It seems to me we *both* win," I said.

Bringing Back the Light

We were in the kitchen, lingering over empty bowls that had held minestrone, watching snowflakes waft promisingly downward and then evaporate upon hitting the muddy ground, when Gail asked "So, are you coming to my parents' on Christmas?"

I shrugged, trying to look nonchalant. "Not sure yet. I appreciate the invitation, but…"

Gail came around behind my chair and kissed the top of my head. "But the commercial holiday with the cast-of-thousands thing isn't too your taste? It's not really mine, either, but it's *my* parents and *my* three siblings and their spouses and their kids. That makes it a little easier." She sighed. "Would you believe Brett's letter to Santa this year was three pages long?"

"Big handwriting?" Brett was her seven-year-old son.

"He used my dad's computer to make sure Santa could read it! And most of the stuff on it is either TV tie-ins or war toys." She shrugged. "What can you do? It's not like I can separate him from the world."

I leaned back against her. "Even if you did, it wouldn't help. When I was Brett's age, my parents were living off the grid up in the Cascades and homeschooling me." Which Gail probably had guessed, me having a name like Yarrow Dragonwind. "My grandmother sent me Barbies and I got hooked on them."

Sophie Mouette

Gail roared with laughter. "Yarrow, admit it! You just loved those big Barbie breasts, even when you were little."

Relieved by the change of topic—and knowing she'd relish an opportunity for spontaneous sex while Brett was safely at a friend's house for the afternoon—I turned around my chair so I could cup her breasts. "If I liked Barbie breasts, it was because I didn't know how much fun real ones were. Especially yours." Gail's weren't exactly Barbie-proportioned, but they were lovely and full on her otherwise small frame. That was nice, but what I adored about them was their sensitivity, how even a light caress would distract her and anything more serious would turn her brains to mush.

It was always fun, and sometimes it was damn convenient. Right now I really didn't want to talk about Christmas with her family.

It's not for the reasons you might think. After Gail's disaster of a marriage, they were so delighted to see her with someone who made her happy that they'd have welcomed a fire-breathing three-headed Martian if it were good to Gail, let alone a harmless granola dyke. And all of Gail's relatives whom I'd met were genuinely nice and eager to make me feel like part of the family.

If anything, that made it worse. I could have handled a holiday soap opera in the role of The Queer Daughter's Dicey Girlfriend. But the idea of spending Christmas with a close family made me want to hide under my duvet with a pile of hankies and not come out until spring.

Concentrating on making Gail writhe in sexual ecstasy seemed like a much better plan than working myself up into a panic. But even that pleasure only took me so far.

Her hot, responsive body distracted me nicely for a while. I tongued her nipples until she begged for mercy, then pulled her jeans off, knelt between her legs and savored the smoky, spicy delight of her until she cried out. She came squirting as she often does, splashing onto the kitchen floor, and I laughed and used her shirt to wipe it up. But when she went to recip-rocate, I couldn't lose myself in the sensation. Perched on the counter, I felt her clever hands and tongue doing things that would usually work like magic. Instead of getting all juiced up, though, I found myself getting more and more melancholy.

Finally, Gail noticed that, while I wasn't exactly crying, my eyes were at least as wet as my pussy. She stopped what she was doing and just held me. I wrapped my arms and legs around her, pressed my face against her shoulder and just shook. I couldn't really cry. It had been too many years and I had cried myself out. Crying would have been easier.

Finally I could talk. "I hate Christmas," was what came out.

"Something to do with your parents?"

I nodded. "You know they died in a fire when I was in college, with my little brother. It was Christmas night—that's the part I don't usually tell people because it bothers them too much. And Oak was…"

Gail did the math. "He must have been about the same age as Brett. Okay, I can see why you hate Christmas, and why Christmas with my family is scary."

"It was never a holiday we celebrated, so I don't even have good memories to balance the horror. It's just the day my whole family died."

"You must have some good memories of this time of year. What about Winter Solstice—Yule?"

Gail hadn't been raised pagan as I had, but it was some-thing she'd become interested in since we'd gotten together. She embraced the principles of it, but was still learning about the rituals and the history. Just yesterday we'd discussed the pagan origins of Christmas, agreeing that the Christian holiday itself had been almost buried in a snowstorm of commercialism.

I sighed. "That one's got *too* many good memories. The last Yule was almost perfect. We did a beautiful ritual out in the snowy woods behind the house, and then came inside and lit candles everywhere and exchanged gifts—we never gave big presents, just some small thing that would be meaning-ful—and stayed up until dawn to praise the sun's return. Only I was a little distracted because I had a new girlfriend and was leaving the next day to spend the rest of break with her in Eugene. The house burned down while I was digesting my first Christmas dinner."

She shook her head, kissed me again, and pulled away from me long enough to put on tea water and let us both get re-dressed. By the time we were snuggled on the living room couch, tea in hand, I was composed again, trying to pretend my meltdown didn't happen, and ready to apologize when it was clear that Gail wasn't going to let me ignore it. "It was almost fifteen years ago. I don't know why it's affecting me this much…"

She set down her cup and took my free hand between both of hers. "What did you do on the winter holidays until now?"

"Hid. Went to the movies, got takeout, found something to read that would engross me. For a few years I took extra shifts at work—they always need nurses on the holidays—but the ER turned out not to be the best place to be. Sometimes I went on vacation to someplace like Martinique or Jamaica, where it didn't feel like Yuletide. I'd like to try to be with your family, for your sake, but I'm afraid it'll dredge up memories."

She squeezed my hand. "What we need," she said, "is to make some holiday memories of our own. I'm going to go make some phone calls."

I must have made some confused noise, because she added, "The Winter Solstice is the twenty-first right? I'm going to get a sitter and we're spending the night at your place. And while we're there, we're going to create a holiday celebration that's ours and ours alone."

*

The day of the Winter Solstice was cool and blessedly clear. Throughout the short day, I'd enjoyed catching glimpses of the mountains in the distance, unshrouded by rain or snow. I'd had to work, but Gail, a teacher, was off for the week and had spent the day at my house puttering. The sun was setting—a rare treat, in Seattle, to see a proper sunset instead of rose-tinged rain clouds—and a pale quarter moon was already hanging low at the horizon when I got home. Gail came to the door carrying a sprig of mistletoe and held it over my head as she pulled me close with the other arm. We didn't need mistletoe, but it made me smile.

When I walked into the house, I gasped. When I'd left in the morning I had a bare Scotch pine in the corner of the living room and that was it for decoration. Bought on Gail's instruction, it was the first tree I'd had in my orphaned adult life. Now pine branches and garlands of princess pine were festooned on the mantle and doorways, covering the tables, even strewn on the hardwood floor. The warmth of the house released their green, fresh-air fragrance. The room was full of unlit white candles—votives in protective glass holders, a nod to my uneasiness with fire. In the center of the room sat the coffee-table altar we'd constructed over the last few days, a simple affair with cotton batting for the snow that would not coat the ground this year, holly and oak branches for the Holly King and the Oak King who battle for the love of the coming Spring, and a bunch of red roses in a gaudy pepper-mint-striped vase because Gail and I both love them and it just felt right. A picture of the two of us was propped against the vase.

On a table next to the altar was the ritual meal we had devised: pomegranate seeds, baked brie with apples, locally made smoked salmon, a bottle of Pinot Noir from a winery we had visited together over the summer, and, in honor of those boar's heads that turn up in the descriptions of old-time Christmas feasts, spareribs and pork wontons from our favorite Chinese place. A chocolate fondue simmered over a candle, the only one already lit in the house. Bright red and white candy canes decorated the areas not covered with plates. It wasn't like any holiday meal either of us ever had (my childhood memories involved a lot of home-canned vegetables), and that was the point. And it was all chosen so we could feed it to each other. The food added its own fragrances to the scent of pine and the faint honey-sweetness of beeswax candles.

"It's so beautiful!"

"No. It's just decorated. You're beautiful." She kissed me again, helping me slip out of my coat. "Go change into something comfortable," she suggested.

I stripped off my uniform and shoes and threw on a loose, comfortable caftan. When I returned, she had poured wine for both of us, as well as some in the chalice on the altar.

"Did you see the sunset?" she asked as we settled on the sofa. I nodded. "I spent some time meditating on it," she said.

"About how short the day was, and how long the night would be. I can understand how our ancestors would have been frightened by the days getting shorter and shorter, and how they felt they needed to have a ritual to bring back the sun."

I nodded, savoring the smoke and berry flavors of the wine. "It made them feel in control."

"Now we have scientific proof of how it works, but ritual is still important in our lives," she said. "Which is why we're doing this, even now. Right?" She stood, extending her hand to me.

"You put it better than I could have, love." I smiled and thought about what she had said. "Because I was raised pagan, it sometimes becomes a reflex to me, like going to church might be someone else. It's all fresh to you, and you remind me what it means. Thank you!"

Together, we lit all of the candles in the room, bringing light into the growing darkness. As we did, we talked and meditated on the wheel of the year. The Solstice heralded the birth of the sun and also the divine son, the savior god. Whether you called him Jesus or something else, the sentiment was the same: a promise of renewal against the darkness and cold of winter.

Soon the room flickered with candlelight. Standing there, in the warm glow, I felt the stress melt away from me as the positive energy of the season coursed through me. This was our night, Gail's and mine. This was *our* ritual. It wouldn't cause the sun's return, but it celebrated the growing sunlight, the inevitable change from one season to the next.

We sat on the floor in front of the food, and fed each other bites: sweet pomegranate, smoky salmon, smooth brie, tangy Chinese, interspersed with sips of wine and luscious kisses.

"I think," Gail said, "we might be better off getting out of our clothes, so we don't drip chocolate on them."

I willingly let her help me out of my caftan, and then I returned the favor, noticing that she had also worn things that were easy to get off. I didn't usually do rituals sky-clad except in high summer—it wasn't practical in the Pacific Northwest and paganism is at heart a practical religion—but in a cozy house with only my beloved there, it seemed like a wonderful idea.

Make that an awesome idea, in the literal sense of the word. In that dimly lit room, rich with evergreen fragrance and illuminated only by candles, the beauty of her body stunned me. "You are Goddess," I whispered, and knelt to press my face between her thighs.

I felt her curl her fingers into my hair, fingers tightening reflexively as my tongue whispered over her clit. So I was surprised when she eased my head away.

"Not so fast," she whispered. "We have all night."

She pulled out the massage cushion and had me lie facedown on it. I purred as her fingers kneaded tension from my shoulders, as her palms lightly caressed my back. I shivered as she moved down to my ass, but alas, she didn't stop there. Her hands trailed to my feet, and I relaxed into her famed, delicate foot massage.

"Tonight's the longest night of the year," she said as her fingers pressed into the ball of my right foot with just the right amount of pressure not to tickle. "The night when we celebrate that, in fact, it *is* the longest night, and the nights will now start to get shorter, and the days longer. When we celebrate the return of the light while savoring the night's own joys."

Her voice was soft, hypnotic, lulling me into a trance.

"Imagine a ball of golden light," Gail continued. "It's surrounding your feet. It's safe and warm, bringing nothing but comfort and energy."

This was a basic meditation, but one I'd usually done alone. It took on a whole new dimension with her hands caressing me.

Those hands, coated in eucalyptus-scented oil, slid around to my ankles, then up to my calves. Gently she massaged the muscles there, all the while encouraging me to envision and feel the peaceful light.

And I did. Meditation has always come easily for me, probably because I learned it so young. It was a simple thing for me to slip into the mental state required, to blank my mind or to fill it with a particular thought or vision. I believed in the lines of energy that encircled the earth, and was able to tap into them. Now, that energy was golden light to me, moving up my body at the same rate as Gail's hands, relaxing and reinvigorating me.

When Gail reached my thighs, I started to tense with anticipation, but she crooned and stroked until I settled down again. It wasn't that I wasn't getting aroused, because I was—it was more that there was no urgency. My clit tingled, but I was more focused on the sensations of the intimate but not entirely sexual massage, and on the light that came with it.

Bit by bit, inch by inch, my muscles lost their tightness. I floated gently, only half-aware when Gail helped me turn over. She massaged my scalp, caressed my temples, worked her way back down. She reached my feet again and, like a good masseuse, didn't abruptly cease contact with me. One hand slid up my leg as she shifted, and I was dimly aware of her curling on her side next to me.

The caress of her lips against mine was blissful. I thought I heard her say "don't lose the light" before her tongue stroked against my bottom lip. Our kisses were soft, sensuous, rather than the almost-frantic quality they often took. How long had it been since we kissed this way, like new lovers exploring each other for the first time? I wondered dreamily. And why had we stopped?

She kissed my throat, tongued the warm sensitive hollow behind my left ear. Her hands, still soft from the oil, didn't miss an inch of skin on my torso, and her lips didn't miss much, either.

My right hipbone became the object of her worship. I had no idea of the nerve endings that existed there, and how directly linked they were to my pussy. She worked with excruciating, but wonderful slowness from there across my belly, teasing the hollow of my belly button until I would have sworn it was glowing from all the bright and loving attention. Then my ribcage enjoyed the same treatment, each usually unregarded inch kissed and stroked.

It certainly wasn't a disappointment when she closed her mouth over my nipple, but it was almost a shock, this move from magical intimacy to something more pointedly sexual. But as she suckled the sensitive nub, I found the magical feeling growing rather than dissipating as I had feared. My whole body was filled with golden warmth, from my hair to my toes, but more and more it was focused between my legs. I was aroused, and my sense of need was increasing, but still I floated in a timeless, trancelike state.

My mind was lost in sensation, but I shifted my hips restlessly as the pressure in my cunt grew, like an expanding ball of light. Then her hand was there, warm and gentle, stroking my lips apart, exploring my wetness. "You are Goddess," she whispered, echoing my words from earlier, "Be thou light." She murmured in delight as she brought her fingers to her mouth, then brought her mouth to my moist core.

The golden glow bloomed within me, then exploded outwards as she brought me home.

"How're you doing?" she asked after sliding back up and spooning her body against mine, one leg thrown over my hips in warm possession.

"All glowy and tingly." Usually after an orgasm, I was happy but ready for round two (or three or…). This time, I felt languid, drifting, still feeling delicate aftershocks tremoring my clit.

"Good," she said, nuzzling her face into the hollow of my collarbone.

Lest you think I abandoned her, I did rouse myself after a long and delightful cuddle and treat her to the same attention that she'd lavished on me. I took the light energy that she'd given me and shared it back with her, massaging and caressing her until we were wrapped together in its glowing strands.

Sometime after that, I remember her pulling the quilt from the sofa over us. That was the last thing I knew until she was nudging me awake.

"Wah?"

"Look, Yarrow. We've brought back the light."

She was right. Through the sliding glass doors that led to the narrow deck, I saw the faintest glow on the eastern horizon. Pale orange tendrils of light parted the long night's gloom.

Something similar stirred within me. I still felt the residual golden glow, and I knew something had changed for me on that long, dark night. Tentatively I reached out and touched the memory of my parents, of my brother Oak, expecting a raw flash of grief. Instead, I found sadness, yes, but a sadness that glinted warmly with love. I missed my family terribly, but they lived on in my memory. Finally, I thought, I might be ready to admit another family into my heart.

Slowly, gently, the wheel of life had turned.

*

In the end, I went to Gail's family Christmas extravaganza. I chatted with her parents, laughed with her siblings, playing with her son and nieces and nephews. They were kind enough to allow me to put a picture of my parents and Oak on the mantle, to be remembered.

I wish my parents and my brother could have met Gail. They would have loved her almost as much as I do. They would have thanked her, if they could, for bringing back the Solstice light in me.

Hidden Treasure

When Brenda was a girl, her widowed mother had worked at Frogmorton House and, promising always to be good, Brenda had been given the run of the estate. She never touched any of the antiques as she wandered through the folly of a Germanic castle, pretending she was a princess in the turreted tower and believing that the narrow servants' staircase was a secret passageway.

When she was older, she fell in love with the romance between railroad magnate Winthrop Frogmorton and Austrian Henrietta Ströbel. Henrietta had claimed the Adirondacks reminded her of her beloved Alps, so Winthrop commissioned her a castle of their very own.

By the time she hit college, Brenda was beyond notions of girlish romance and obsessed instead with history, particularly the Victorian era of upstate NY. When she finally returned and took on her dream job as curator of Frogmorton House, it had been her idea to have the staff dress appropriately, to give visitors the full experience of the *schlöss*-like manor.

She'd never admit aloud that one of the reasons she'd hired Sean as a security guard last month was because she guessed he'd look mouthwatering in a proper Victorian policeman's outfit of dark blue wool.

She'd been right about that. Oh, had she ever been right.

Now, as the lights flickered ominously, she looked up from the computer screen, aware that she hadn't been seeing the membership newsletter in front of her. She'd been fantasizing about Sean again.

Still, she automatically hit Save, just in case they lost power. The battery backup should mean she wouldn't lose anything, but you never knew with computers.

She slipped off her narrow black-rimmed glasses, surprised to see how dark it had become. Had she been woolgathering that long? Somehow, not surprising when it came to thoughts of Sean.

They'd gone to the same high school, but she'd been bookish and involved, and he'd been distant and sporty and a little shy, his bangs always tumbling into his eyes when he ducked his head.

Now his silky black hair was shorter, but tousled and untamed on top. He'd enlisted after high school, he told her when he started work at Frogmorton House, and by God, now that he was out, he was growing his hair again.

He was no longer shy, no longer a boy. His shoulders had broadened; his brilliant blue eyes held depth and experience. His grin was roguish, his stride confident.

And Brenda appreciated all of that. A lot.

She also appreciated the way his wool pants snugged over his tight asscheeks. Her hands itched to cup the muscled curves, pull him close...

Shaking herself back to the present, she flipped on the antique banker's lamp on her desk and glanced at the clock, certain it would be time to close up the House and head home to her thermal lounging pajamas, leftover homemade pizza, and her Welsh Corgi, Mort.

But it was only 3 p.m.

She glanced out the window. All day they'd had menacing grey clouds, as ominous a sign as the flickering lights. She'd known they were due for a storm, and by all accounts it was going to be a humdinger.

She just didn't expect the world to be white already.

The snow swirled down in gusts and eddies, the flakes dancing like manic fairies. She couldn't even see the ever-greens just outside the window.

The lights flickered again, this time going completely out for a few seconds before returning. Brenda saved the membership newsletter file again, copied it onto a flash drive, then shut the computer down. It had been an excruciatingly slow day already, and in this weather they weren't going to get any more visitors. Best to close early and get out before the roads got too slippery.

She grabbed the walkie-talkie off the desk. "Sean, this is Brenda."

No answer.

"Sean? Pick up, please."

She gave the walkie-talkie an exasperated shake. Cell phone service was seriously dodgy in the Adirondack Mountains as it was, but Frogmorton House was nestled in a little valley that defied the reach of any cell tower. Sean should have his walkie-talkie on…

She'd just have to go find him.

Not that seeking him out was such a bad thing. Brenda slipped her burgundy velvet fitted coat over her deep green wool and cashmere dress, glad for the extra warmth—Frog-morton House was drafty even in the height of summer and today's storm was rattling the beautiful but ill-fitting windows, the glass wavy from more than a century of relentless gravitational slide.

She smoothed the velvet down the molded line of her torso. Even on quiet days like this, when time dragged and she didn't get to share her passion for Victoriana with another soul, her job still thrilled her. How many people got paid to hang out in a castle and wear a glorious late-Victorian outfit, complete with corset, to work?

Plus, a well-made corset was incredibly comfortable. Not to mention the pleasing way it nipped in her waist and plumped up her breasts.

She'd definitely noticed Sean ogling her cleavage.

Sean could ogle her cleavage any time. Do more than ogle, if it came to that, which she hoped it did.

During his interview, his sensual lips had curved into one of his roguish grins when she mentioned the required policeman's uniform and the formal butler's outfit he'd don when he helped at fundraisers.

"Bonus," he'd said. "Halloween every day. I always loved… trick or treating." His tone was light, but his voice deepened suggestively on the last words and hit straight between her legs. She felt herself flushing and bit back an urge to offer all sorts of treats (and an assortment of tricks), right on the spot.

Thank God Hank, their bookkeeper, been looking down at Sean's résumé at that moment; his proper elderly brain would have caught fire from the looks shooting back and forth between them.

The heated glances and flirtatious remarks had been piling on ever since. But they simply hadn't had time to do anything about it. First the series of Victorian Christmas teas for the local school kids, and the holiday fundraising cocktail party (Sean had made the kind of butler who'd have had real Victorian matrons consorting with the lower classes in a heartbeat), and then getting the house undecorated, and getting year-end thank-you letters out in time to make the IRS happy, and trying to sort through the Whitney bequest…

Plus all the maintenance issues that kept Sean busy because, face it, a lot of the time there wasn't a lot for a security guard to do except just be there, but the house itself could devour all your time if you let it. And like Brenda, Sean would let it.

One more reason she liked him.

She left her office, which was in the parlor off the foyer so she could hear when tourists arrived.

Frogmorton House's pale stone hearkened to its Austrian and German inspiration, and it had round towers and clusters of narrow windows and a meandering, wandering layout that didn't make a whole lot of sense, really. The unconventional design made the House seem vaster than its two-stories-plus-basement-and-unfinished-attic. From the outside, it looked like it should be the setting for a ghost story or a Gothic tragedy, but Winthrop and Henrietta had lived into chubby, philanthropic old age, surrounded by a passel of children and grandchildren who, unusually for the era, had all survived to adulthood. The place was homey as well as grand, with a large nursery and elegantly framed children's drawings proudly displayed next to the Sargent portrait of Henrietta.

Brenda loved the place with an unholy passion.

She found Sean emerging from the basement into the kitchen. His dark hair was mussed—then again, it always had a mussed look to it, like he'd just crawled out of bed, and that was a lovely image because then he'd probably be naked—and a few cobwebs clung to the crisp navy blue wool of his uniform. The brass buttons shone as if he'd just buffed them, though.

"There you are," Brenda said. It was sort of a stupid thing to say, but for a moment there, the spicy smell of his aftershave had glued her tongue to the roof of her mouth. "I was trying to reach you, but the damn walkie-talkie…"

"Needs new batteries, I think," he said with an apologetic smile. "I'll pick some up tonight. But if you wanted me to check the fuse box, I just did. Replaced the fuse for the left tower, but the rest survived the power surge okay. Fuses. Sheesh. You wouldn't have an electrical upgrade scheduled any time soon?"

"It's tricky with a historic house—and expensive." She shrugged. "Maybe after we reslate the roof so it stops leaking into the Birch Bedroom." Frogmorton House was luckier than many small museums—some of the numerous Frogmorton descendents had inherited Winston's generous spirit and knack for business—but money was still a constant struggle.

"Maybe we should check out the Birch Bedroom, make sure it's not snowing in there?" Sean raised one heavy dark eyebrow in a way that would have done a movie star playing a wickedly naughty hero proud. If Brenda had any doubts that his mind was in the gutter—and she didn't, because hers had descended right along with his—his smile made it clear he wasn't thinking about protecting the William Morris wallpaper or the delicate dressing table.

"Oh, no," she blurted. "That bed frame's already damaged."

Oh God. She felt her face suffuse with heat. Had she actually said that aloud?

Yes, and despite the rush of mortification, she couldn't say she regretted it.

Not from the look on Sean's face, which had gone from flirty-but-work-safe to something that wasn't safe anywhere, and certainly not at work. Especially not when your work-place boasted seven bedrooms, six of which had sturdy, comfortable, downright decadent Victorian beds.

Heat coiled from her flushed face, tickled her nipples, spread down to her sex, which pulsed in appreciation of the images racing through her mind. Her. Sean. One of those Victorian beds—not the one in the Birch Room, which was only a single anyway, but maybe the grand canopied Frogmorton matrimonial bed....

Her lace-trimmed silk drawers caressed her thighs as she shifted nervously back and forth, rubbed against her suddenly damp and sensitive cleft. The corset held her like an embrace.

Her nipples felt like they were drilling through the now-confining corset.

Sean took a step forward.

The lights flickered again as the wind let out a howl like a tortured soul.

In the brief darkness, Sean's arms slipped around her, pulled her close.

His lips brushed hers. Soft, an inquiry, but with the promise of so much more behind them. He smelled good, like bay rum and something slightly musky that she thought was just him.

They'd kissed once before, back in high school when Brenda had been inexperienced and she guessed Sean had been, too. He hadn't gone to the prom, but crashed the party by the lake. Of course there'd been drinking. At some point she'd turned on the log where she sat and he'd just been *there*, and their lips had touched, and then he'd eased back and for a moment she saw the fire reflected in his eyes, and then he was gone.

Sophie Mouette

He kissed like a man now, and she was woman enough to appreciate it.

She had a dim memory, however, that she'd come to find Sean for reasons other than snogging him, but damned if she could remember what they were. She'd been thinking about his sculpted mouth for a long time, and it felt just as good on hers as she'd imagined.

Better, even.

The lights came back on all too soon, though, and with it, some semblance of reason.

Damn.

She licked her lips, aware of how provocative the action was by the way Sean's nostrils flared. "Uh…don't know if you've noticed, but the snow's coming down pretty hard. I'm declaring us closed on account of bad weather."

Suddenly serious, he nodded. "Plan. Do you want to ride back into town with me? At least if we get stuck, we won't be alone."

Brenda's Outback was fine in snow, but he did have a point. Being alone out there if something went wrong would be Not Good. If it had been anyone else, she might suggested he just follow her so they could keep an eye on each other—get both cars back to town, all that.

But she liked the idea of a ride home with Sean. More to the point, she liked the idea of asking him in once they got there, and having him meet the dog, share the pizza, maybe open a bottle of wine—and see if they could build on the promise of that kiss. "Sounds good. You lock up the back. I'll grab a few things from the office and meet you out front."

Brenda made sure everything was shut down, changed the message on the answering machine to say they were closed, and grabbed her flash drive. The one thing she'd wanted to get done this afternoon she could do at home just as easily (assuming she didn't let Sean sweep her off her feet, that is).

Very little of what Mrs. Whitney had left the house was directly useful—some Victorian-era family photographs and papers and a few nice pieces of furniture. But some of the more modern stuff looked like it might be collectible and she'd been combing eBay and other auction sites, looking for information.

Good God, that wind was terrible. She swore it wasn't just rattling the windows, but penetrating the stone walls.

Then she looked out the window.

Damn.

The world was a solid wall of white.

She went to open the front door. It opened a crack and then stopped. Too much snow piled in front of it.

Double damn.

"I think we're stuck."

Sean's voice made her jump. He'd snuck into the room; when she turned, she saw he was in his stocking feet, as if he'd left wet, snowy boots in the kitchen. Snow clung to his pant legs, all the way to his thighs.

Normally the idea of snow on the irreplaceable and already worn peacock rug would trigger her anal-retentive tendencies, but it was hard to get into full preservationist mode while staring at Sean's thighs—the snow was almost up to his crotch. The carpet had survived several generations of Adirondack winters, when various Frogmortons had presumably tracked in snow on a regular basis. It could handle a little more.

"You can get out through the kitchen door," he added, "but the snow's knee-deep—or worse—already. We could dig my

Jeep out, but we're not going to get far. Even if they're keeping up with the main roads, no one's touched Frog Hollow."

She picked up the house phone. "I'll call the plow guy. Maybe he can push us up on the schedule. Assuming his cell phone's working." Frog Hollow Road was private, more like a long driveway than an actual road, and they had arrangements with a neighbor with his own plow to keep them dug out.

The plow guy answered his cell, all right—from the hospital, where his wife was in labor. ("Great timing, eh? I can already see this kid's gonna be trouble.") He had back-up, but she had a day job to get home from and her own plowing clients to hit. "Best make some coffee and get…"

A loud crackle made Brenda jump and hold the phone out from her ear as if it was a live mouse.

When she moved it gingerly back to her ear, it was dead.

Well, wasn't this interesting? Snowed in *and* incommunicado.

On one hand, poor Mort was stuck home alone—she just hoped he'd have the courtesy to do his business on the tiled bathroom floor when he got desperate. (Or better yet, that the next-door neighbor who'd walked Mort for her when she was working late would be clever enough to notice she hadn't made it home and come to the poor dog's rescue.)

On the other hand, she'd daydreamed about spending the night in the romantic old mansion. Spending the night in the romantic old mansion with a devilishly handsome man was an even better idea.

Especially a devilishly handsome man who'd already kissed her once and showed every sign of wanting to kiss her again. And more.

Oh yeah, especially more.

The next gust of wind was so hard she half expected the stained glass window sporting the Frogmorton utterly ridiculous faux coat of arms (which included, perhaps unsurprisingly, a frog salient, or leaping) to blow in. Which would be a shame. Fundamentally tacky it might be, but it was part of the house's history.

"It's warmer in the kitchen," Sean suggested. "And that's where the coffee pot is."

"And the food. We might as well use the microwave before the power goes out. Because face it, the power *is* going to go out."

Sean took her hand. "Oooh, I'm scared of the dark. Will you protect me?"

"Jerk." She smacked him playfully on his ass (his very fine ass). But she didn't let go of his hand while she did it.

And when he took advantage of that fact to reel her in for another kiss, she decided that inconvenience and potential carpet-cleaning and all, being snowed in was just fine with her.

His lips were warm, but his cheeks were cold from his foray outside, a contrast that made Brenda shiver with delight.

The first kiss had been tentative. Questioning. This one started that way, too, with feather-light brushes and tiny flicks of his tongue against her lips like snowflakes against bare skin, only hot.

Brenda was more than happy to encourage him to the next level.

She threaded her fingers into his hair, which was damp from the snow, and boldly deepened the kiss, meeting his tongue with hers and then dipping farther, between his lips, to find the sweetness beyond.

A sharp intake of breath. His body tensed. Then he leaned in, his fingers massaging the muscles just inside her shoulder-blades as he pulled her closer.

This version of the kiss sent tingles right down to her toes and back up to where they mattered the most.

The lights flickered again, actually going out for enough time to plunge them into darkness, where the only thing that existed was the feel of him touching her, mouth to mouth, chest to chest, thigh to thigh, and a delicious hardness of his pressing against the softness of her lower belly.

Power restored itself, with no promises of how long it would remain, or whether the next time would be The Big One. It took all of Brenda's willpower to pull away from Sean enough to say, "Um. We'd better get something to eat while we still have electricity."

Sean's grin was fiendish, and they were halfway to the kitchen when it occurred to her that he'd interpreted "something to eat" in an entirely different way from how she'd intended it.

It was her turn to grin. Oh, she liked the way his mind worked.

*

When Jeremy whined "It's *co-old*" for the third time, it was all Clyde could do not to undo one of his snowshoes and smack it into his friend's kisser.

"It's not that bad," he said for the third time. "I heard once that when it's really cold, it can't snow. All this snow means it's not really cold."

"I don't get it," Jeremy said. "It snows in winter, and it's cold in winter. Snow is cold."

Clyde didn't understand it, either, but he'd lived in the Adirondacks for all twenty years and three months of his life, and he'd noticed that sometimes it was colder when it wasn't snowing, so cold the hair in his nose froze up.

It wasn't *that* cold right now, a fact for which he was quite grateful.

The snow fluffed and fluttered around them, and poofed up beneath their snowshoes. Their breath lingered in the cold air like pot smoke in the shed behind the high school.

"It's not my fault you didn't dress warmly," he snapped, finally giving in to his exasperation. He regretted it almost immediately when he saw Jeremy's face fall.

Still, he couldn't keep from adding "Like I told you to."

"I didn't know it was going to be this *far*," Jeremy protested.

Apparently Jeremy had thought they'd be driving to Frogmorton House, as if they were going to make a triumphant entrance and demand the property that was rightfully Clyde's.

Clyde didn't think that would go over well with the people who worked there.

"It's no farther than the deer blind on the other side of Cascade," he pointed out.

Jeremy heaved a sigh. "But we have *beer* stashed there."

"I will buy you a case of Pabst when we get back, I swear," Clyde said.

A smile crossed Jeremy's wind-red face. "Really?"

"Cross my heart," Clyde said.

Mollified, Jeremy started off again. Really, the long underwear top and down vest and jeans should keep him warm enough while they were moving. Clyde felt almost too hot in his own layers, which included a checked red-and-black hunting shirt and thermal socks his grandmother had given him last Christmas.

God rest her soul.

Then again, it was all his grandmother's fault he and Jeremy were out in the middle of the woods right now.

She may have gifted him with thermal socks, but she'd denied him his birthright, and as God was his witness, he was going to claim what was rightfully his.

Before or after he pitched the whining Jeremy into a ravine.

*

Sean put on a pot of coffee to brew while Brenda explored the fridge and cabinets for something resembling a light supper. The rich aroma made her mouth water as she set out her findings.

Bagels and cream cheese left over from a Chamber of Commerce breakfast. A frozen pizza stashed by Sean in case of a dire lunch emergency. Energy bars and green tea drinks. A handful of ketchup packets—not at all useful right now. A tin of instant hot chocolate with mini-marshmallows. (Possibly dessert.)

Best of all, far back in a cupboard, a dusty bottle of decent champagne left over from some long-past benefit. Brenda tucked that into the fridge for later.

She'd always believed in thinking positively, and positive thinking right now included the idea that by the end of the evening, they'd have something to celebrate.

From the pantry she dug out a pair of the nothing-special-but-looked-properly-historic heavy silver candelabra they used for parties. Soon candles were flickering over on the counter, making the kitchen both cozy and romantic. She hadn't intended that.

Okay, maybe she had. Just a wee tiny bit.

Sean had his flashlight at the ready, too. But when the power went out for good, they didn't reach for the flashlight. They reached for each other.

The candle flame sent Sean's cheekbones into sharp relief, made his eyes just that much more deep before he pulled her in for another kiss.

First little nibbles on her lower lip that made her shiver with delight, but set a fire deep inside her. Shivering but hot. Nice.

Her lips parted, and his tongue brushed the inside of her mouth, exploring the surfaces, sparking more delicious sensations.

Once again, she laced her fingers in his hair, holding him as if he might escape. Not that he was showing any sign of wanting to escape.

Sean kissed away from her mouth to her ear (which made her giggle, even though it tickled in a very, very sexy way), to her throat, until his lips were brushing against the handmade lace ruffle just at the base of her throat.

Sean found an extra-sensitive spot on the side of her neck, half-hidden by lace. When she moaned, he seemed to decide that lace and a little bit of wool were tasty enough as long as he could reach her through them.

More shivers. More fire. Throbbing nipples and a pussy that pulsed in time with her heart.

Pure need.

Damn, why wasn't she wearing her ball gown? Sure, she'd have been freezing with her arms and cleavage bare, but it would give him so much more skin to touch and kiss. She pressed herself against him, trying desperately to feel more of his body. It wasn't easy through layers of skirt and petticoat— she'd gone for the layered effect because it was both authentic and warm, but damn, right now she was regretting it. As much as she was regretting her authentically high neckline.

Her hands slid down his broad back to his ass, cupping and gripping it, pushing him closer so she could push herself against the hard bulge in his crotch.

Not enough. Not nearly enough.

He slipped a leg between hers and still it wasn't enough contact.

It wasn't just the fabric in the way, although that was a problem. She wanted to feel his skin. No, she wanted him inside her skin—inside her, yes, but under her skin too, and she under his.

At the very least, she wanted to start unbuttoning his crisp uniform jacket—but she'd have to pull away to give herself room to work, and that would mean less delicious contact.

Decisions, decisions.

"Too many damn clothes," Sean said, barely lifting his mouth from her skin. "I love the way you look in the Victorian outfits, but they get in the way."

"They do come off, you know."

He pulled back enough that Brenda could see his face. His grin was even more wicked by candlelight. "A little at a time, though. We've got all night, and I'm getting off on seducing the lady of the mansion…who quite likes slumming it with a policeman."

She resisted the urge to note that in the Victorian era, *slumming* referred to counterfeiting.

Resisting had less to do with actual thought than with the way Sean's big hands slipped her velvet coat off her shoulders and then went to work on the tiny buttons on her bodice.

He paused to run his fingertips lightly over the top of her breasts, where they swelled over the corset. She gave up on thinking altogether and just felt.

*

Clyde stopped. Jeremy went right on by him before he realized it, and stopped as well, scootching backwards carefully.

"What is it?" Jeremy asked.

Clyde jerked his head, indicating forward. "There it is." As if Jeremy couldn't see it.

Dusk had fallen. The air was the midnight blue of twilight, when everything seemed possible. Around them, the wind was the only sound. The snow still tumbled down.

In the gloom, the house loomed before them like the opposite of something out of a bucolic Christmas movie. Clyde had expected to see some lights on, even after the staff left, but the entire place was menacingly dark. He was glad he had a Maglite in his backpack.

"Whoo-ee," Jeremy said. "Crazy-lookin' place, ain't it?"

Since the land around Frogmorton House was owned by the museum trust, there was no hunting on the premises, but their usual hunting grounds skirted the area, so they were familiar with its bulk.

Even though hunting season was long past, Clyde had brought his shotgun, just in case. Never know when you might come up against a bear, grumpy at being woken early from its hibernation.

"Guess they went home early," Clyde said. "Better for us, anyway. Won't have to wait."

Jeremy rubbed his hands together, his ski poles dangling from straps around his wrists. "Can't wait to get my hands on some treasure."

Clyde tossed him a silver flask. "I'll drink to that," he said.

*

Sean moved from the left nipple to the right, drawing it into his mouth, making her arch so he could take more in.

The bereft left nipple puckered in the cool air, pressing against the slightly damp linen of her corset cover. He didn't let it get cold for long, though, tweaking it between his thumb and forefinger.

Tit for tat—or was that tit for tit? Brenda pinched his nipples, which stood out dark behind the not very Victorian, but eminently practical white t-shirt he wore under his uniform.

True to his word, he was taking his time. Her dress was open to the waist, but he decided he liked the lace-trimmed corset cover and had worked her breasts above the corset without taking it off. And while her skirt was pushed up, showing off her silk drawers—she was perched on the kitchen counter at this point, with her legs wrapped around Sean's waist—he wasn't rushing to get the drawers or his pants off, either. (Although, thank goodness, he'd taken off his gun belt—that had been a little distracting.) Never mind that he was hard as a steel rod, threatening to pop the fly buttons on his trousers, and never mind that her drawers were so drenched in the crotch that they must be transparent, or that they were both trembling with want.

When was the last time someone had taken the time to explore her this way? Never, not that she could remember—and Brenda was damn sure she'd remember it.

Remember being this aroused, this sensitized, so much so that Sean's breath on her skin felt like a touch. Remember being this wet and open and needy. Remember her sex pulsing around emptiness, yearning to be filled. Remember reaching for a fly with an achingly hard cock behind it and being turned away with a playful reproach and a passionate kiss.

Her mother always said patience was a virtue.

And in this case, Mom was right—up to a point. But damn, if Sean didn't pick up the pace, she might catch on fire.

"I want to be naked with you," she whispered, running her hand down his chest and taut belly to his fly. One of the relatively few brain cells that wasn't focused on her rising need pointed out that there might be a better location for doing so than where they were. Someplace with soft surfaces and warm blankets. "And not on the kitchen counter, either."

"Spruce Bedroom?"

The master bedroom with the fully made-up bed, very comfortable bed including an impressive, if perpetually dusty, embroidered velvet coverlet and canopy? "Hell yes." The sheets were Irish linen, still sturdy despite their age. And if by chance they destroyed them, well, it would be a shame, but they had an entire closet full of similar sets.

Before she hopped down from the counter, he cupped her mound at last, and that pressure was almost enough to drive her over the edge.

Almost. Not quite. "Please?" she moaned, feeling ridiculous to beg but needing it so badly that she didn't care.

His grin grew. He looked like a fox, or maybe it was just foxy. Delicious, in any case. "I like hearing you beg."

Brenda writhed under his hand. "Please. Pleasepleasepleaseplease…"

He started circling his fingers, slowly but with just the right pressure. "Yeah. That's it. Perfect…so close…"

She took a deep breath, sensing that within seconds she'd need it to scream.

And in that instant of silence, they heard the distant sound of shattering glass.

She might have thought she imagined it, except that it was followed immediately by the shrill droning of the burglar alarm.

*

Jeremy jumped back as if the house had bitten him. He started to run—and promptly fell down because in his panic, he forgot he was wearing snowshoes. It would have been hysterical except for the alarm screaming at them.

"Clyde! There's an alarm!"

"Asshole. Of course there's an alarm. And you just tripped it by breaking the window."

"Then how were we going to get in?"

Honestly he'd been hoping that there wouldn't actually be an alarm, but he wasn't about to admit that. But he did have a plan. He reached into his pocket. "I have instructions! How to disarm an alarm system."

"Really? Where'd you find that?" In the last of the fading light, Jeremy finally looked interested.

"On the Internet. You can find all kinds of shit on the Internet." It occurred to him belatedly that he'd never tried them out and they might be just as fake as the boobs on a porn site.

What the hell. The window was broken anyway, the alarm was going off. Might as well just crawl in the window the old-fashioned way. If the alarm was sending a message to the police station, well, the cops couldn't get there before morning at least, and by then they'd be long gone.

He propped his rifle against the wall and leaned down to remove his snowshoes. Then he shimmied out of his backpack and tossed it inside before clambering in after it.

It was, of course, pitch black inside, but he got the flashlight on just as Jeremy fell through the window and landed with an audible thump.

*

"Just a broken window," Brenda said, hoping Sean would put any quiver in her voice or shake in her hands down to sexual frustration.

Which was definitely part of it. Whatever this emergency was, the timing couldn't have been much worse. Although maybe it wasn't all bad. She'd probably feel even more anxious if every nerve in her body wasn't too busy screaming for relief to register the influx of fight-or-flight hormones.

"It's really windy," she added. "Probably a branch or a roof slate or something blew through." She was buttoning every third button of her bodice as she spoke. Getting them all would take way too long, but she'd be damned if she'd face down an intruder—or even deal with a simple, drafty, broken window—with her tits hanging out.

"Let's hope." Sean fastened the gun belt around his hips, grabbed his big flashlight, then gave her one last quick, hard kiss. "You stay here. I'll go check."

"No way. I'm going with you."

"I'm the security guard. It's my job."

"And it's my museum, dammit."

"Your museum?" He glared at her, his thick eyebrows drawing together. He did *fierce* awfully well for someone with such a gorgeous smile. But not well enough to make her back down.

"I'm responsible to the board for anything that happens… and I know this place like the back of my hand. Better than you do." She took a deep breath and decided to admit to the truth. "And if I have to sit here alone, I'll go nuts. I'll leave any tackling of burglars up to the person with combat training, but I can't just sit here."

Sean nodded. "Good points, all of them. Let's go." He headed for the main door.

She shook her head as she grabbed the candelabrum. "Servant's hallway. If there's anyone in the front rooms, we can surprise them coming that way. And shut off the damn alarm while we're at it."

*

They'd made it to the front of the house. Clyde poked his head in one room, but it was being used as an office, and he didn't see his target.

"What are we looking for again?" Jeremy asked.

Something resembling a brain in your head. Clyde gritted his teeth. "My grandmother's writing desk. You remember, the one that used to be under the window in her living room."

"I don't remember," Jeremy said, as if he hadn't sat in that living room a million times eating Clyde's grandmother's homemade peanut-butter thumbprint cookies like he was one of those starving kids from Africa.

"It was kind of a reddish wood, with carving along the front—roses or something. Stood about this high." Clyde held out his hand, palm down. "She usually had a vase of fresh flowers on it, and a framed photo of my grandfather."

Jeremy squinted. "Okay," he said finally, reluctantly, as if he maybe didn't really remember but he didn't want Clyde to get angry.

At Christmas a few years ago, Grandma had gotten tipsy on eggnog and told Clyde something very, very important.

She'd told him the desk contained a special treasure.

When he'd asked what sort of treasure, she'd smiled a smile he'd never seen before (and even though he couldn't quite explain why, it kind of squicked him out) and patted him on the head and told him he'd understand one day. And Clyde had taken that to mean that she'd be giving the treasure to him.

Then she'd upped and croaked and left everything to Frogmorton House, including the writing desk—which, as far as he was concerned, they could keep—and the treasure she'd promised him.

"We'll split up," he said, because Jeremy had done one thing right and remembered to bring a flashlight of his own. "You go upstairs; I'll look down here. Look for anything that looks like the desk I described. We'll meet back here in—" he checked his watch "—fifteen minutes."

He felt compelled to add, "Don't break anything else. Don't even touch anything," as Jeremy clomped towards the stairs.

He shone his own flashlight left and right. Right seemed to be the dining room, and he doubted the desk would be in there. Left, then.

At the top of the stairs, he heard a bang and an "Owdammit!" from Jeremy. Then Jeremy's faint voice wafted down, "S'okay! Didn't break anything!"

Clyde went left.

*

As Sean fiddled with the alarm box, Brenda leaned out the broken window, careful not to brush against a fragment of glass. "They came on snowshoes," she announced. "Two pairs. There's a rifle out here, too."

"Good to know they didn't bring it inside," Sean commented into the blissful silence left when the ringing stopped.

"They could have another one," Brenda said. She stepped back, her shoes crunching on the glass. She was pretty sure the window hadn't been an original, but she was still pissed off that the slobs had broken it.

"We'll cross that bridge when we come to it."

They continued on. At the end of the servants' hallway, in the dining room, Sean signaled a halt.

Brenda halted all right. She felt a little ridiculous with her long gown and her candelabrum, like the ditzy heroine of a vampire movie.

At least she wasn't going to make the ditzy-vampire-movie heroine mistake and run off on her own. Face it, neither the Master's in history nor the certificate program in non-profit management had covered How to Deal With Intruders.

"Flashlight," Sean whispered, making almost no sound at all. She had to lean in to hear him, which brought back the scent of—oh God, *herself* on his fingertips. The reminder of her arousal made her clit tremble again.

"What was that?" she whispered back, sure she'd heard something.

"Voices. Couldn't hear what they said. I think you're right: there's two of them."

"Good odds," Brenda said, even though she wasn't much sure she was a match for one of them. She'd been desperately trying to remember the self-defense course she'd taken in college. That had been a long time ago, and she and her friends had spent most of the time ogling the instructor.

Why hadn't she paid attention? Nobody said she'd actually *need* that information being a curator.

"Stay behind me," Sean said. In any other circumstances she would have gladly done so just to look at his ass, but now she actually paid attention to the matter at hand.

They crept through the dining room and entered the foyer just in time to see a faint light moving away from them, towards the sitting room and library.

Sean had loosened his jacket so he had easier access to his gun, but he left it in its holster. Brenda hoped he wouldn't have to use it.

She was appalled that someone would break in. Yes, the place was brimming with antiques, but most of it was heavy furniture. The knickknacks were all discretely marked and everything, down the silver, was obsessively categorized and photographed. If the thieves tried to sell anything, they'd get caught, no question about it.

Sheer mindless vandalism, then? It wasn't out of the question, but it didn't make a whole lot of sense. They usually had problems on the 4th of July or around graduation time, when stupid kids got stupid drunk and came up with stupid plans.

Surely nobody was stupid (or drunk) enough to want to come out here in the middle of winter, on *snowshoes*, just to smash things up.

The snowshoes, Brenda decided, meant they'd planned this.

That made her even madder. She felt like a mother partridge puffing up to protect her young.

Although didn't mother partridges pretend they were wounded to draw predators away from their chicks? Might not be a bad strategy here, if it came to be needed.

Following Sean, she was impressed at how smoothly he slipped through the rooms. Victorian decorating called for a lot of furniture to be jammed into small spaces—and don't even mention the knickknacks and lace and frippery. It was all utterly lush and romantic, but it made it hard to walk in a straight line.

Sean moved like a panther, lean and silent. And Brenda knew where every stick of furniture was placed better than she knew her own apartment.

The man (she assumed it was a man) they followed, on the other hand, had neither of their skills. He wasn't crashing into things, at least, but he was moving slowly and bumping into the occasional side table, chinking the curios and ornaments against each other.

At this rate, they could have followed him blindfolded, just from the noises he was making.

They caught up with him easily in the vaguely leather-scented library, which had looped them around almost back to the foyer. Brenda had the vague sense that they could have just waited for the perp to come back to them, but it was too late to contemplate that now.

"Freeze!" Sean shouted.

Brenda jumped. She pressed a hand to her pounding chest as the thief whirled and his hand shot into the air. His flashlight made crazy patterns on the ceiling.

"Don't shoot!" he said.

"What are you doing here?" Sean demanded, training his own flashlight on the thief's face.

Wait a minute... Brenda stepped from behind Sean, squinting in the gloom.

"*Clyde*?" she said. "Clyde Whitney, is that you?"

Clyde started to bring his hands down, but Sean's sharp "Hey!" made him re-think that. "Yes ma'am, it is."

"What in God's name are you *doing* here?"

Sean shot her a look that clearly said, *Who's in charge here?* but she ignored him. The situation was back in her territory now.

"It's Clyde Whitney," she told him. "His grandmother left Frogmorton her things when she passed. I know him from when I subbed at the high school. You graduated two years ago, isn't that right, Clyde?"

"Yes ma'am."

"So why are *you* here?"

"The things my grandmother gave you," he said. "She wasn't supposed to give you everything. The treasure was supposed to be mine."

Treasure? "What treasure?"

"In the writing desk. She *told* me."

"I'm sorry, Clyde, but I think she was mistaken. She gave us a detailed listing of everything she was donating, and she didn't say anything about something being in the desk."

Clyde let his hands drop, not threateningly, but as if he'd forgotten he'd been caught. "But—"

And that's when they heard the voice behind them. "Clyde, I think I found it! It's in the big bedroo— Oh, crap."

The speaker loomed right behind Brenda. Without thinking, she turned and nailed the stalker across the head with the heavy silver candelabrum.

The young man blinked once, then crumpled to the floor.

Most of the candles went out, but one dislodged and went flying. With a shriek, Brenda dove after it, stomping out the flame before it caught anything alight. She winced at the thought of wax on the hardwood floor, but she knew several different secrets to removing it.

Then, in the near-darkness, she ran her hands over the candelabrum to check for any dents or nicks. It may have been an everyday one, but it was still a part of Frogmorton House.

"Nice job," Sean said, admiration in his voice.

She straightened her coat. "Thank you."

Sean gestured to Clyde. "Come on."

Clyde's eyes widened. "Where are we going?"

"You two can cool your heels in the basement until morning. The cops won't be able to get here 'til tomorrow, and we can't let you go off tramping around the countryside."

"What about my treasure?"

"There's no treasure," Brenda said.

"But—"

"But we'll check the writing desk, just in case. Okay?"

"Okay." Clyde's shoulder's drooped.

Sean made Clyde help him lug the half-conscious and moaning Jeremy to the basement. Brenda grabbed an armful of wool blankets from the linen closet. It would be chilly down there, but they wouldn't come near to freezing to death.

*

In the light of the freshly burning candelabrum, Brenda found the secret compartment in the back of the writing desk within minutes. Sean whistled his admiration.

"I never thought to check for a false back," she said. "Hello, what have we here?"

She drew out a packet of papers, tied with a red ribbon and smelling of cedar and lavender.

She examined the envelopes. "They're letters," she said. "From Mr. Whitney to Mrs. Whitney, and vice versa."

"Love letters?" Sean said with a chuckle. "Grandma's secret treasure was her love letters? Aw, that's sweet." Then he smiled, and it wasn't the roguish, flirty grin that Brenda had come to lust after. It was a softer smile, still sexy as hell, but almost…wistful.

So, naughty Sean was a closet romantic? Brenda told herself firmly it was too soon to obsess about the ramifications of *that* bit of information—although they could be very nice ramifications—and filed the knowledge away for future reference.

She'd meant to take a quick glance at the letters, then put them away and get back to more interesting matters, but the first few lines she read intrigued her so much that she kept reading, not even bothering to sit down.

"Oh my. Not just love letters. *Steamy* love letters. Listen to this." She scanned the letter until she found the passage that had caught her eye.

"'I miss you. All of you: your eyes, your laugh, your toes, that mole on the back of your leg, your beautiful breasts, your round little bottom, and every other bit of you. But right now, I really miss being inside you, feeling you so tight and wet and hot around me. When I get home, I'm going to kiss every inch of you, from your forehead to your cute painted toes'—hmm, seems Mr. Whitney was a bit of a foot fetishist—'and then I'm going to lick you until you beg you to fuck me. But I don't just want to fuck you. I want to make love to you. I want to make love to you so we can't tell where I end and you begin.'"

Brenda looked up. Sean's eyes were shining, dark blue and wide.

"Hot stuff," he said. "As long as I don't think about Mrs. Whitney playing bridge with my grandmother, at least."

"Let's not go there, okay?" Brenda laughed. "God, Clyde would die, knowing we're reading his sweet old grandparents' smutty letters. Hell, knowing his grandparents *wrote* smutty letters."

Brenda shuffled through the papers. "Here's another good one. 'I know I'll be home in a week. I may even get home before this letter gets to you. But a week's too long. When I'm alone in my hotel room, I take out my cock and play with it, trying to pretend you're touching me instead, imagining your hands, your lips, your sweet, greedy cunt. And I come. Oh, do I come. But even while I'm coming, all I can think about is how much better it is when I'm making you cry out and tighten around my cock. Do you touch yourself and think of me? I'm sure you do, because you're a naughty girl and that's part of why I love you so much, but write to me about it. That way, the next time I travel, I can read it and imagine you lying in the dark touching yourself and imagining it's me.'"

"Did she?" Sean asked.

"If he was half as sexy as he sounds in these letters, I bet she did. It looks like he traveled a lot on business."

"I mean write him about it." Sean had moved in behind her now and was reading over her shoulder while he unbuttoned her dress.

Brenda leaned back against him as she flipped through the packet. "Found it! 'You want to hear how I keep from going crazy while you're away? You want to know how much I miss you? I miss you so much that my fingers aren't enough sometimes. I can make myself feel good that way, but it's not the same without you inside me. I hope they're feeding you well in Indianapolis, because you're going to need your strength when you get back here.'"

"Lucky man. I bet he got a warm welcome home."

Sean pushed against her as he spoke. Even through her layers of skirt, Brenda could feel how hard he was.

It pretty much matched how wet she was getting again, between the steamy letters and Sean's hot body pressed against hers and the memory of their play down in the kitchen.

"It gets better. 'It got so bad that today I went to the market and found a cucumber about the right size. It wasn't the same at all, but filling myself up with something made it easier to think of you inside me. So imagine me so desperate for you that a cucumber looks pretty good. Imagine me pushing that cucumber in and out of me and calling your name and…'"

She stopped. "I actually can't read the rest because…well, it looks like he did imagine it. Often. This letter's pretty beat up."

Sean let out a shuddering breath. "Jesus, that's hot. Just knowing she was so horny and so far away must have made her husband crazy." He pushed her dress off her shoulders, forcing her to set the letters down on the desk so he could work the narrow sleeves down her arms. "Have you ever been that horny?"

She turned in his embrace, letting the dress slither off her hips as she did. "Not until tonight. And it's all your fault. Hope you're planning to do something about it."

Another of those rougish grins that made her insides quiver and melt. "I don't know…I kind of like the idea of watching you getting yourself off." He paused just long enough to get her concerned about the evening's plans, then added, "Sometime, if you'd be into it. Not tonight. Tonight I want to be inside you when you come. Want to feel you exploding all over my cock."

Brenda slithered the rest of the way out of the dress and got her petticoats and corset cover off in record time.

Sean stopped her when she was down to corset and drawers. "Let me look at you," he breathed. "Just for a minute. Damn, you look good like that."

She made a show of unpinning her hair, shaking it out so it tumbled around her shoulders. "No fair. It's cold. Besides, I want to see you, too."

"Fair enough." He opened his fly teasingly, one button at a time. The purple head of his cock peeked out the top of his purple briefs.

She couldn't resist. She sank to her knees and kissed it before working the trousers and underwear down.

Enough teasing. Enough playing. She wrapped a hand around the base of his cock and took him in her mouth.

Salty and delicious and just the right size, thick and meaty. Perfect to suck and even better to fuck.

Sean groaned as she moved her lips up and down his shaft. God, she wanted this moving inside her, filling her, making her scream. She wanted to milk him so he exploded inside her, wanted to come and come and come on this delicious cock, but damn, he tasted so good it was hard to resist continuing to suck.

He was the one, in the end, who pulled away. "Let me help you with the corset," he said huskily, "and get on the bed. I want to be in you."

She was already turning around so he could reach the laces, even as she teased, "I thought you liked the corset."

"I do, but I want to feel you. See you. The corset's sexy. But you're gorgeous."

It wasn't necessarily easier having him help with the corset—she'd gotten good at managing on her own and it seemed to be new to him—but it was certainly more fun.

Onto the bed then, with a mountain of covers pulled over them, the linen sheet cool underneath her and Sean lying over her. Like Mr. Whitney had promised his bride, he kissed his way down her body—suckling her nipples until she moaned and rolled her hips with need, exclaiming over the corset marks on her hips and belly and licking them "to make them better."

He reached the reddish curls of her mound, buried his face there, took a deep breath as if enjoying the bouquet of a fine wine. Brenda made a small noise, half crazy with arousal, and put her hand on his head.

She didn't think he'd needed the hint, but he certainly took it.

Brenda didn't have time to enjoy a full demonstration of Sean's oral skills, though—after the long tease and the hot letters, a few flicks of his tongue were all it took to send her into convulsions of pleasure.

There was a brief interruption while Sean fished a condom out of his wallet. (She was amused—and a little relieved—to catch him checking the expiration date on the packet. He might be sexy as hell and a big-time flirt, but he hadn't needed the "just in case condom" in a while.) Even with the interruption, she was still twitching with aftershocks when he repositioned himself between her legs, the head of his cock pressing against her pussy.

He'd said he enjoyed hearing her beg, hearing her admit just how much she wanted him. And since she did want him, and the hotter she made him, the hotter she got, and so on, she opened her legs a little wider, rolled her pelvis, looked into those amazing blue eyes, and whispered, "Please. Please fuck me."

"Sure you wouldn't rather have a cucumber?" He pressed against her as he said that, teasing at her already sensitized clit with his head.

She smacked him on the ass. To her surprise, the yelp he let out sounded awfully happy. "Sounds like you liked that."

He shook his head, a bemused look on his face. "I think I did. Who knew? We'll have to talk about that. Later. Much later."

He pushed into her slick pussy, just the head at first, giving her a few seconds to appreciate how thick he was, how delicious he felt there, how much she wanted to feel more.

Wonderful as the long teasing had been, she'd have to be superhuman to be patient any longer. She raised her hips, grabbed his ass, said "Now," and gave him a push all at once.

"The lady desires something?" he purred, and slid the rest of the way in.

He froze, buried to the hilt inside her. His eyes widened, looking impossibly bluer in the flickering candle light. His mouth opened. He looked like he was striving to make the perfect clever, wicked remark, but couldn't find words.

Then he started to move.

Oh God did he start to move.

He was like the blustery weather outside, fierce and elemental and inexorable. He was howling like the storm and cutting through all her defenses like the wind cut through the walls. He was wild and dangerous and beautiful as the snow. But he wasn't cold. In the freezing room, he was fire, and she was burning with him.

After his earlier delicacy and restraint, he was letting himself go crazy now. Each stroke jarred her to the core, but in the most pleasurable way, raised her up off the bed and threw her down again. Each stroke touched someplace new, someplace wonderful, sending another wave of icy-hot ecstasy out to drown her. The storm was raging and she was raging, gouging at his back and ass with her nails, urging him to fuck even harder even though if he did he'd break her in two or at least break the antique bed.

She came, and it didn't end. Not multiple orgasms, because that implied stopping at some point and then starting again.

This was one long spiral of pleasure, rising higher and higher without respite, without conclusion.

It was almost too much, but at the same time it wasn't enough.

It wasn't enough until Sean's face, already red, contorted to something beautiful but scarcely human, some god or nature spirit, maybe the face of the storm itself. "Yes...Brenda..." he cried and she almost didn't recognize her own name, but she recognized the way his muscles clenched and released, the way that even with the condom between them he seemed to surge into her.

They fell asleep tangled in each other and woke to early light peeking between the velvet drapes. Brenda crawled reluctantly away from Sean's warmth, wrapping herself in her velvet coat, to look out onto the white world. The snow had finally stopped, but it didn't look like they'd be going anywhere for a while.

Not that she minded (although she'd be happy when the police could come out and take charge of the two idiots in the cellar—maybe she should toss them some bagels). Sure, the house was chilly, but she suspected she and Sean could find ways to keep warm. Something about watching her play with herself, for one, and something about spanking him, for another. They could probably make the spanking go both ways, because she was curious about being on the receiving end herself. So many possibilities—and for once, so much time.

And now, in the light, they could really see each other.

Brenda crawled back under the covers, snuggled close to him and kissed him on the shoulder. "Wake up, sleepyhead."

"I was awake. I was just about to roll over and grab you when you got up."

"It's a beautiful, cold, snow-covered day and it looks like we're stuck with each other."

"Aw, damn. Whatever shall we do?" He rolled over and grabbed her, and for a few glorious minutes there was nothing but his body, his mouth, and his clever hands.

Then he stopped, pushed himself up on his arms and looked down at her. "Brenda, I have a confession to make."

She froze. She couldn't tell if he was serious or not, couldn't read the dense blue velvet of his eyes, couldn't read what lay behind the sudden absence of his usual grin.

The silence lasted longer than she liked. Finally he spoke. "I applied for the job just knowing it was for a security guard."

Brenda nodded. It had been a blind ad; she knew because she'd written it, hoping to get at least a few applicants who weren't dreamy kids who just wanted to work at the "castle" and would fall apart at the first sign of a real problem.

"But I took it because of you."

Gulp.

"I had another offer, from a resort out by Blue Mountain Lake. Paid better and I could have lived onsite. But after I saw you again at the interview, I knew I'd have to take this job and then ask you out like I didn't have the nerve to do in high school."

"I refuse to believe you pined for me since high school."

The roguish grin came back. "Not exactly. But you intrigued me, and I thought about you. Wished I could go back in time with what I'd learned since then and sweep you off your feet—or at least really get to know you. So when I got a chance, I took it. Plus you grew up really nicely."

"You too." Brenda breathed an inner sigh of relief. "At least we both had ulterior motives. So I don't have to worry about a sexual harassment lawsuit?"

A snort. "No way. But I hope you don't mind if I harass you for sex every chance I get."

She grinned. "It's only harassing if one of us doesn't want it. And I don't think we'll have that problem. So what kind of harassing for sex did you have in mind this morning?"

He stretched. "I'm not sure yet. So many possibilities. I know—why don't you grab those treasure letters and we'll see if we find anything inspirational?"

About the Authors

Called a "legendary erotica heavy-hitter" (by the über-legendary Violet Blue), ANDREA DALE writes sizzling erotica with a generous dash of romance. Her work—which has been called "poignantly erotic," "heartbreaking," and "exceptional"—has appeared in 20 year's best volumes as well as about 100 other anthologies from Soul's Road Press, Harlequin Spice, and Cleis Press. She finds passion in rock music, clever words, piercing blue eyes, the wind in her hair, and the scent of the ocean. Visit AndreaDaleAuthor.com for more information.

TERESA NOELLE ROBERTS writes sexy, magical tales for lusty romantics of all persuasions. Her work appears in *Best Bondage Erotica 2011*, *2012*, and *2013*; *Carnal Machines*; *Best Erotic Romance 2013*; and other provocatively titled anthologies. Look for contemporary BDSM romances and the paranormal Duals and Donovans series from Samhain. She loves Yule, Christmas, and any other excuse to celebrate in the dark of a New England winter. Visit TeresaNoelleRoberts.com for more information.

Author of the 4-star (Romantic Times) novel *Cat Scratch Fever* and many short stories, SOPHIE MOUETTE is the brainchild of two widely published authors of erotica, romance, and speculative fiction. The two halves of Sophie—Dayle A.

Dermatis (aka Andrea Dale) and Teresa Noelle Roberts—met more than two decades ago at a writers' conference. Talking nonstop, they closed down the hotel bar and went somewhere else to keep on talking. Although they've always lived on opposite sides of the country (and for a few years, on opposite sides of the Atlantic), they've remained very close friends, and it was only natural that they should start writing together as well. Visit SophieMouette.com for more information.

Also by Sophie Mouette

Novels

Cat Scratch Fever
Out of the Frying Pan
Possessed, Undressed, and in a Mess

Short Stories

Catalyst
Don't Move
Dyeing for Her
Hidden Treasure
Sacred Places